T0196219

Boy
Genius

(And Other Possibilities)

SONYA FALLS

authorHOUSE®

AuthorHouse™
1663 Liberty Drive
Bloomington, IN 47403
www.authorhouse.com
Phone: 1 (800) 839-8640

Published by AuthorHouse 01/20/2017

ISBN: 978-1-5246-5999-8 (sc)
ISBN: 978-1-5246-6000-0 (e)

Contents

Boy Genius

The room was clean, desks straightened in rows, bulletin boards trimmed in autumn leaves, and welcoming, inspiring posters had been placed strategically throughout the room. Parents had answered the call of "Open House" in record numbers and Nadine felt by 7:15 as if she had greeted all 750 of them.

She stood, straightened herself to her full 5'10" frame and moved to the open door in order to get any breeze that might make its welcome appearance from the hallway. It was a typically hot August night and as usual, Open House was held after school hours in order that working parents might drop in with their disgruntled offspring, chat with their young person's teachers, pick up schedules, and get a start on the new school year. Of course this was the best time for these meetings, but it did not coincide with the air conditioning timers which cut off promptly at five o'clock. Never mind asking for a resetting of those timers. "Well, the air is on a timer and if we have to reset it, you may not have air tomorrow. This thing is set in Greensboro, you know, we don't mess with those guys" was the central office mantra to endless requests to *Please* let us have some air during Open House!" Nowadays Nadine had quit complaining, wore lots of deodorant and had lately resorted to visiting her friend Berkley in the science department where they both swathed their inner thighs with corn starch. "Preparing for battle" Berkley called it. It really did absorb a lot of moisture.

As the steady stream of parents and surly, sometimes sheepish students had begun to recede, Nadine thought she might take a few moments to straighten her stack of "Classroom Policies and Curriculum Guides" and to tally up the total of visiting parents. This had to be turned in to the office by tomorrow morning in order to be filed away for the spring visitors from SACS who always wanted to know about the "partnerships between parent and school." She was just beginning to put in the last number of "50 parents, 27 students" when *she* entered the door, towing behind her a gangly, raven-haired child of 13 or 14.

Nadine had been expecting *her* all night, but in the press of many parents and students, she had forgotten about her possible arrival. Now here she was,

1

arriving at two minutes until 8 o'clock and sure to keep Nadine well after the end of Open House.

"Open House be damned," thought Nadine. "I'm going to tell her that it's over and we can meet some other time...I'm...." But she knew this would not happen because *she* was Mrs. James Ronald duShane III and (which had to be her fourth and thank God for birth control), her last child, James Ronald duShane IV. Mrs. duShane gracefully swept to a halt in front of Nadine, all 110 pounds of her, blond hair expertly tied back with a natty little bow, her crisp blouse and tiny little skirt looking so cool and neat. No sweat on her brow and I'll bet no cornstarch either, thought Nadine, catching a whiff of very nice perfume. She stopped herself before snuffling like a horse for a deeper sniff. Stop it! she told herself, forcing a smile and extending her hand.

"Mrs. duShane, I've been expecting you and James. I saw his name on my Honors English roster and knew that you would be coming by. Hello, James."

James hung his head and looked at the floor while his mother graced Nadine's large hand with her rather small, soft one.

"Hello, Nadine. Yes, I'm running a bit behind. The children's hospital committee ran a little late tonight and as chairman, I had to be there. I had called Mr. Martin earlier this summer about rescheduling Open House but he said something about this night being sacrosanct or something, I can't remember, but anyway, here we are! We are all so excited that James is going to be in your English class. After all, you have taught them all, and I want my little Jamie to have the same opportunities as his brothers. As I have often said, those who sit at the feet of Socrates will..."

"Well, come right on in, and have a seat," Nadine interrupted this flow of nonsense and gestured to the little duo of desks that she had pulled up to her desk for the night. Mrs. duShane slid gracefully into one of the student's desks and James fell quietly in the other one. Nadine had long ago given up trying to fit in the students' desks. It could be done, but it wasn't one of her finer moments. Nadine sank into the chair behind her desk. Safer here, she told herself.

Mrs, duShane brought her Gucci purse up to rest before her on the desk, clicked it open. What is she doing? wondered Nadine. Make up? Lipstick? Nothing needed doing that she could see. Suddenly, three dollar bills were retrieved and handed to James. "Jamie, sweetie, could you go to the cafeteria and bring me a soda? I didn't have time for dinner tonight, Nadine. Can you find your way to the cafeteria?" James, who had been looking at the motivational posters in the back of the room, mouth gaped open (adenoids, thought Nadine) slowly turned to his mother and in doing so, caught Nadine's intent gaze. He blushed, drew his chin back to his neck, and left the room in two long, loping strides, the bills clutched in a knobby adolescent fist.

Mrs. DuShane watched her last-born leave the room and whispered, "I didn't want him to hear what I have to say to you. I don't think he needs to think of himself as being any different from the other children." She looked Nadine squarely in the eyes. "Nadine, I'm going to save you the trouble of looking at Jamie's records tonight. You know me, you know my family, my other boys, but this time, Nadine, you are in for a real treat. James, this child-my baby-is without a doubt, a certifiable genius." She paused for a few seconds to let that little gem sink in with Nadine.

"Oh, I know what you are going to say-all mothers think their children are geniuses. But I never did, not with Tony, Robert, or Andrew. They were smart, brilliant boys at times, but they are not one-eighth as smart as this one. James is bound for great things, Nadine, I just know it, and now, you are going to experience it this year. I have seen the signs all his life. A soon as he could walk, he was exploring things the other boys never noticed. He would study the lock on the dishwasher and try to figure out how it worked, the pattern of flagstones on the patio fascinated him for hours, and his *reading*! He was reading **The Cat in the Hat** at 24 months! Now, I'm not telling you this to alarm you or have you treat him any differently from the other students. His brilliancy will shine through and I'm sure that his influence on the other children will be a help to you each day. I swear, Nadine, this year is going to be your best!" Mrs. duShane sat back in the desk and looked expectantly at Nadine.

Inside, Nadine cringed. She thought briefly of the previous duShane boys, not an original thought among the three of them, but avid readers. If James was anything like his brothers, it would be a long year with her begging for homework to be turned in, for reports to get finished, with countless calls home, and a matching number of excuses from this woman sitting before her as to what activities the boys had had to engage in that prevented them from completing the work *which in her opinion might not have been challenging enough for Tony, Robert and Andrew to begin with.*

Enough! thought Nadine. I've suffered enough. End this now. Twenty-five years of smiling, agreeing, nodding, and cajoling lazy children had to stop. Have the decency to tell her that she is mistaken, that James is NOT a genius, that he is probably only a notch above the village idiot, that he will not do stupendous things, that if he gets out of high school with a diploma, he will be lucky...Tell her! Tell her! Steaming devils hissed inside Nadine's head and caused her to feel dizzy and her mouth to fall open.

"Mrs.duShane, I...." Nadine stopped because James re-entered the room at that moment with two cans of soda, the condensation gathering on the red and silver cans in iridescent beads. He thrust one toward his mother who sat daintily in the desk, still waiting for Nadine's response to her revelations about genius.

"Here, Mom," he spoke quietly, almost inaudibly. The other drink he handed to Nadine. Her fingers closed around the can, and she murmured her thanks as the cold wetness filled her body and spirit with relief. "I had enough money for another soda, Mrs. Miller. I thought you might want one, too. I know you've been here all day." James looked shyly at her as he pushed a lock of dark hair off his forehead.

The soda was delicious, its dark, sweet message burning and cooling her throat all the way to her stomach. What an intelligent kid! Nadine surmised, her previous condemnations drowned by the brown nectar, her wrath beginning to ease under the pleasure that only a carbonated drink could provide. She studied James' face as she smothered a small burp and bit her tongue. *To hell with the truth. She doesn't need to know and* you *are a judgmental bitch, Nadine, who has taught school too long.*

"Well, James, you mom has been telling me quite a bit about you. What have you read? Are you a sci fi lover like Andrew? I'll bet you like Poe. I think he was Tony's favorite. All that gory description! Of course, you'll have your own favorites. We'll start the year with *The Odyssey*. Are you familiar with that?" Nadine handed him a "Classroom Policies and Curriculum Guide" as she led both mother and child to the door, her arm companionably around James' hunched shoulders. "Nadine," one smoldering devil whispered in her ear, "you are a weak-kneed pushover-bought for the price of a cold drink!"

"Ah, shut up!" Nadine answered back silently. "What do you know? It could happen.....*a boy genius*... in my class...WOW."

Peace at Any Price

(Author's Note: In 1977, NASA successfully launched two spacecrafts, named **Voyager** *I and II. Their purpose was to explore the outer planets, Jupiter, Saturn, Uranus and Neptune. Since that launch date, vast astronomical information about these planets has been relayed back to the scientists who created the crafts. No one knew how far the crafts could travel or how long signals could be sent. However, in 2013, something even more extraordinary happened.* **Voyager** *I burst through the heliosphere, the bubble that separates our solar system from the other galaxies. Truly, incredible things could now happen. What follows is the story of one of those possibilities.)*

None of the "messages" understood when it had happened. It seemed plausible that it occurred sometime after their craft *Voyager* had burst into interstellar space, that uncharted region 100 astronomical units from Earth. Nor did any of them understand *what* had happened. They only knew that solitude was no longer possible on the craft. To say that things had come to life would be a misnomer since nothing on board had ever *had* life. Perhaps a better description would be that the messages had become "engaged".

It could be stated that all the messages needed was a leader, something to tell them what to do. On the other hand, it could be argued that there were too many voices telling empty space what to do. Fifty-five voices in fifty-five languages speaking greetings, instructions, and introductions over and over again became clamorous. Add to that the alternating sounds and images of earth as had been recorded on the Golden Record and the confusion and noise was deafening. Of course the images took up no space in the decahedral shaped vehicle. They simply flitted about, bouncing off the ceiling and fading away only to return a second later so that sprinters collided with a group of children, the Great Wall of China, as well as Ms. Goodall and her beloved chimps. The sounds of rush hour traffic, a loud tree toad, as well as a Chinese dinner party were overlaid with all 27 selections of music that had been sent to show the culture and sophistication of earth's inhabitants. Instead, the bedlam that filled the spacecraft would have convinced anything that encountered it that Earth was a level of hell. A leader, if one could be found on board, would probably not be able to control any of it.

Man's Image had recently begun to "sense" that a peaceful place existed and he sought it often. Named fittingly enough, "Monument Valley", he had found it vividly depicted on the Golden Record. As often as he could escape from Woman's Image, which held his hand too tightly, he transferred his one dimension to Monument Valley and entered into the heat and nothingness which soothingly poured from the Record.

Although M.I. could not think for himself, in the blessed tranquility of Death Valley, he found that he could experience sensitivities here that were not possible anywhere else in *Voyager*. Before the "engagement", he had never felt this need. He hadn't really *felt* anything. But now, this place gave him something, some *vital* thing that he wanted: peace and quiet as it had been before "things" had taken form. He wondered if Woman's Image possibly felt this same need to escape, although she never came to Monument Valley. At least he never saw her there. Or rather, never felt her there. He, and she, had lips, noses and mouths, but the ability to speak or communicate had never been a possibility until now. As Man's Image became aware of Woman's Image, her shape and face, he began to want her to desire the same things he had begun to feel, especially the peace of Monument Valley. Without warning, Woman's Image clutched his hand again and he sensed a return to the clangor of the ship.

M.I. shifted his attention from W.I. because the din had grown to unbearable decibels. M.I. thought he would try to tell W.I. about Monument Valley. He began to communicate using the pressure of his hand, thumb and fingers, often making small circles and designs on her palm. But she interrupted his description to tell him that she, too, had been to an exciting place. She had just found it on the Golden Record and had asked it to show itself to her. It was called a *music room* and didn't he want to listen? She seemed very happy and her hand trembled in his. He found this happiness infectious. He pressed her hand to signal yes and suddenly, he was bombarded with hundreds of different types of music all playing at once and all very, very loudly. The vibrations alone were enough to fill M.I. with horror. *Madness. Absolute madness.* M.I. transferred back to Monument Valley with a sigh of relief. If he could just stay *here*....

The craft continued on its way. Time meant nothing to the images on board. The spacecraft was destined to travel 40,000 years before encountering anything or anyone. That warring voices, sounds, and images were not in tune inside *Voyager* could not be an issue to anyone back on Earth. (Communication with the vehicle had stopped once the craft entered the heliopause.) It certainly meant nothing to the emptiness of space, but to be rid of this chaos began to mean everything to M.I.

To make matters worse, W.I. had begun to enjoy pitting musical groups against each other. She would have one group perform for awhile and then select a group from a totally different musical genre to play or sing. Neither could bear to hear the other and would begin to play or sing before the other was finished. Their only weapon in this challenge seemed to be volume and each participant employed it to its highest pitch. W.I. vibrated wildly when she hosted these meets. She most enjoyed pitting *Johnny B. Goode* by Chuck Berry against Beethoven's *Fifth Symphony*. *Johnny B. Goode* always won. W.I. would clap her flat palms and vibrate happily.

M.I. never stayed to hear these chaotic clashings, of course, and retreated to his Valley. Lately, however, he had found himself not alone. The French Message had also begun to seek out the solitude of Monument Valley, and perhaps in keeping with his human nationalistic creators, he never came to the Valley without an opinion. M.I. found him petulant and whiny. He wished that he had a voice and could tell French Message to shut up.

"Oh, M'sieur Man's Image," French Message would begin, "you do not know what agony it is to have a voice. No one listens to me. British Message is such a snob, German Message I refuse to acknowledge, and the American! Such idiocy he speaks! 'We come in peace. We are from the United States of America!'" Snorts would follow this tirade. "As if it is not obvious where he is from, or that any creature out here would care! I tell you they are all a pack of nincompoops. I abhor them! If only my creators had sent me a companion-someone with the grace, the charm, the intelligence that is inborn to the French! Someone... like me!" His condemnations would last for hours until M.I. tuned him out and fell asleep. When he woke up, French Message would still be there but he would be silent. M.I. sensed that he was miffed, but at least he was quiet.

Desperation began to enfold M.I. *He had to escape this place.* One day after being hounded into Monument Valley by the French Message and W.I. begging him to listen to "just one round" of the Australian Aborigine songs having it out with Stravinsky's *The Rite of Spring*, he decided that something had to be done. He knew that instructions on the origin of the spacecraft, how it was flown and landed were in symbolic form on the Golden Record.

He would interpret the symbols, land the spacecraft and simply get off. W.I. could go with him if she wished. He didn't care one way or the other.

M.I. spent all of his time now searching through the Record's images, symbols and messages. He had almost given up when suddenly he found the sought for description. Labeled simply "Landing Instructions", he spent a long time figuring out the symbols, arrows, and dots. He had consulted charts of the area through which they flew and had selected a small dot in the heliopause which might be a planet or a particle flung from a dying star. He didn't care what it was. It would be for him a final destination, and he dared to hope, one of silence. He sat back, pleased with his decision. He would be master of his domain, no Message to bother him, no music to listen to, and above all, no noise. A feeling of peace settled over him as he pondered his departure. He would ask W.I. if she wanted to go with him. It seemed only fair since she was supposed to be his partner.

He found her vibrating intensely to some rather awful pan pipes and Chinese gongs. He grasped her hand but she signaled to him to wait until the "music" had ended. Finally, after some spine-shattering clangs of the Chinese gongs, she turned her flat face to him and signaled, "Yes, M.I., what is it? Did you like those sounds?"

"No, W.I., no, I did not. Listen, I am landing this craft. I'm getting off. I can't take this noise anymore. I've found a fragment that looks promising for landing and I am leaving. I think it's only fair that I ask you to go with me, since you are of my species. Do you want to go with me?"

W.I.'s hand became perfectly still. Of course, it would be confusing to her, M.I. realized. He would give her a moment to digest the request. The smaller hand clenched and unclenched against his palm. Finally, she signed, "What will be there? Are you sure it will be safe? Is it cold? Could I take the music messages?"

M.I. signaled with frantic speed, "Absolutely not! They are one reason that I'm leaving, W.I.! I thought you understood that they are unbearable to me. No, they cannot go."

"Then I can't go with you. I'm not sure what we would be getting into. Besides, I enjoy vibrating to the music messages. You should try it sometime."

M.I. sighed. "I have tried, W.I. I...I have no rhythm in the...the foot area."

She signaled a laugh with her thumb. "M.I., you should stay with me. It's what our creators had in mind that we would arrive together as examples of our species. If I go alone, what will our receivers think? That Earth was occupied by females only?"

"I don't think our creators thought that the "engagement" would take place. That is what ruined everything, and frankly, my dear, I don't give a damn, what our receivers think. Tell them whatever you want. Draw a picture of me. That's all they were supposed to get anyway." He withdrew his hand from hers and crossed his arms as a means of ending the conversation.

Immediately, M.I. began landing preparations from the craft. As he had suspected, the Messages were very upset and began to reprimand him in all 55 languages. It was so distracting that he almost missed the particle's flat landing surface which would have put them all on a tall, pointed mountainous structure. *Voyager* sat down smoothly, in spite of the shouting Messages which alternated between curses, pleas to "go slowly", or prayers to various gods. Even their collective sighs of relief upon landing were too loud for M.I. Together the sound reached the level of a F5 tornado.

M.I. opened the hatch at the top of the craft and climbed out to sense his new home. He clambered eagerly down the smooth side of the ship and stepped flat footed onto the rocky surface. Never able on *Voyager* to experience temperature, he welcomed the cold surface. What was cold anyway? It made no noise. He gyrated in excitement, as he swaggered forward, aware of a singular, beautiful thing: It was quiet, so quiet, you could, as some might have said, hear a pin drop. He relaxed and absorbed the perfection.

Something touched his elbow and he turned. He felt W.I.'s presence before he felt her hand seeking his. Perhaps she would stay. Perhaps, in a way, he hoped that she would.

"It's very cold here, M.I.," she signaled. "I don't see how you will bear it."

M.I. shrugged. "It is cold, but it is quiet. It is…tranquil. It is what I need. Will you stay?"

She signaled *no* with her little finger. "I need you to tell me how to get the space craft flying again. The Russian Message is trying to take over inside and I am really fearful of what he might do. There is such coldness in his voice." She shivered.

M.I. sighed. He felt a bit of sympathy for her, but nothing would dissuade him from his plan. "Use the launching instructions on GR 15, track 5. Tell the Russian Message that China wants to talk to him about a weapons exchange. He gets very excited about relationships with the Chinese Message. And keep French Message in Monument Valley. He could cause trouble. Good luck, W.I." He pressed her hand in farewell.

She returned the pressure and signaled, "To you, too, M.I. If we find anything out there, I'll try to come back to check on you. It's the least I can do." M.I. felt her stepping away from him.

He raised his hand in farewell and watched her climb back into the ship. He waited until he heard the giant resuscitation thrusters gain power and lift the spacecraft quickly into the air.

He stood very still for a few moments and then began walking, soundlessly.

April Foolery

If dogs could plot, seek revenge, plan an April Fool's prank, what would it be? Would it be directed to their masters or other dogs? And would a dog know that April 1 was coming up? Would he have time to make plans, to buy the fake doo doo, to switch water pans, or anoint the forbidden sofa leg? I've known few dogs who would have enough pocket change to purchase many objects for April Fool's nor many who had the inclination to plan. However, I'm sure that those dogs exist. Actually, I picture a perky, energetic little Jack Russel taking part in such a daring spring adventure. Yes, yes, I can see him clearly...bouncy little boy, full of mischief and daring....Ah! There he is!

Hang with me now; let's follow this little dog awhile and see what he can get up to. Let's name him Hercules, perhaps because of his strong voice and combative leaps into mid-air.

Hercules lives on the corner of Titan and Woodbine Streets in a small town. He is an only dog owned by a young couple who have put off child-bearing for awhile in order to try their parenting skills out on this small brown and white bundle of energy. Needless to say their efforts to manage, nurture and control their young charge has been, well, fruitless. Jack Russels come with their own ideas of education and Honey and Lonnie have come to the conclusion that while dogs are nice, they do require a lot of patience and love. They tell themselves privately that Herkie has been more than they bargained for.

Hercules usually begins his day with a turn outdoors to take care of the usual morning chores that all dogs enjoy. He leaps from the back porch, lands squarely in the middle of the walkway and runs madly around his yard barking wildly. If there are miscreants hiding in the lilac bushes, Hercules will rout them out and they will think twice about returning to hurt his family.

Panting and growling, Hercules then circles his favorite pee tree, the maple in the right front yard. Circling, circling, circling he finds just the right spot on the trunk and sprays a healthy stream, after which he vigorously scratches the ground with his sturdy little back legs. That will deter any other dogs from desecrating his territory.

Now, since it's April Fool's and we have decided that Hercules has the wit and the will to pull a prank, I would suggest his planning would begin now as he trots to the back porch and lies down. He takes up his morning position, front paws hanging off the top step, tongue lolling out of his mouth and brain churning at phenomenal speed. He runs through the acquaintances of his life; who has mistreated him the worst? Howitzer, the Irish setter next door finds it great fun to hold him down with one great auburn paw and lick his face. The mailman curses him under his breath each day as Hercules jumps higher and higher trying to bite the hand that dares to invade his mailbox. There's that mean kid, Robbie, who throws a small rock over the fence at him each day as he walks to school. Hercules would love to get out, just once and become the ankle biter that he knew he could be-just once! And Robbie, the stone-thrower, would never, *ever* walk on his side of the street again.

Hercules closes his eyes in order to concentrate better. Who, who was worthy of his prank? And what would the prank be? He sighs deeply. From inside, he can hear his owners arguing about, as usual, who will clean his water bowl and put food on the porch for him. Neither one wants the task and it is the topic of yelling each morning.

"You're the one who wanted that dog!"

"No, I did not! Your mother gave him to you just to torment me. She knew I didn't like dogs!"

Yatter, yatter, yatter it went every morning. Hercules hurts inside. Why couldn't they love him and appreciate his attempts to guard them and the house? He stays in the yard all day and keeps up a ferocious tirade of barks at any moving thing. What else is a dog to do? Suddenly, he sees his prank. They obviously didn't want him-he would pretend to be dead. Then they would be sorry. Yes, that was it! He sits up on his haunches and smiles wickedly. He knows just what he will do. When Lonnie comes out to get in his car, Hercules will burst out the gate and run into the traffic, hide behind a car on the other side of the street, yelp with pain and play dead! It was so simple it was silly.

"Bye, Lonnie," shouts Honey. "Don't forget to keep Hercules in the yard!" It is time for action. Hercules bounds off the porch and darts under the shrub at the bottom step. Lonnie hurries down the walk way, opens the gate and Hercules is right behind him. He is out! Oh, the freedom of entering the street! Those singing tires! The honking horns! It is so exhilarating! Lonnie's scream of "Hercules, come back!" Herkie barely hears as he dashes in front of an ambulance, snaps at the rear end of a Volkswagen and makes it to the other side where he yips loudly and falls in a heap (well out of the traffic) on the opposite sidewalk.

Lonnie holds up his hand and stops two cars on his way to Hercules' aid. Hercules holds his breath and curls his lip back from his teeth. (He had seen a dead dog once and that was what he had remembered about the poor beast-his lip curled back.) Lonnie leans down and picks up the little dog.

"Herkie, Herkie, you poor thing! Why did you do that?"

Hercules thinks he hears Lonnie sob. Good, he thinks. Serves you right. He feels himself being carried back across the street and into the kitchen. He is lain on the counter.

"Honey, come quick! Herkie got out and was hit in the street. I think he's dead!"

Honey rushes into the kitchen and looks closely at her dog. Hercules tries to stiffen his legs. She pokes a finger into his belly.

"Dead is he? Little bastard. Little yapping bastard. Well! Can you bury him before you go to work?"

Lonnie straightens up and stares at his wife. "Certainly not! You know I have to be at work by eight o'clock! What can we do with him?"

"Well, I don't know. I'm not digging a hole this morning or tonight. Let me get a plastic garbage bag. I think I can get him in the deep freeze."

Hercules hears her move toward the pantry. The deep freeze! Heavens, no! This has gone far enough. Hercules' eyes fly open, he snorts and struggles to sit up on the counter.

"Well!" exclaims Lonnie. "Look at that. He's alive! Must have been in shock! Welcome back, old boy! You're a tough little joker, aren't you? Isn't he, honey? A tough little joker!" He rubs Hercules behind his ears and gives him a hearty pat on the back. Hercules gives himself a good shake and licks Lonnie's hand.

Which all goes to show that April Fool pranks hardly ever turn out like you plan, but they are all better than a turn in the deep freeze.

Clambake

"I had a peach of a wife," our host announces suddenly. "She never complained or nagged. I would take these trips to New Hampshire to hunt, stay out all night, and she never said a word. Next morning, she'd be up, fixing my breakfast. Never a word about how late I was or nothing." He shakes his head. The old tub had been pulled off the fire, still half-full of little necks, and haddock wrapped in foil. "We fixed too much," he says. "When my dad used to have a clam bake, we never had nothing left." He smiles across the table at me, the son of that dad now an older man himself, white chest hair peeking out from his open-necked shirt. "We used to invite half the neighborhood, me and my wife, didn't we, Deb?"

Yeah, Pops, agrees his daughter.

I want you to come to a real New England clam bake, he had said. My daughter is coming down and bringing a half a bushel of little necks. As so she had, and so we went.

We sit under a tent, safely out of Hurricane Charley's dribbling remains and share a clam bake, complete with sausages, potatoes, good sweet Jersey corn, lots of beer, and some drinks of a stouter nature. We sit afterwards, full of butter-drenched clams and he speaks again of The Peach.

"And she never asked me for nothing, either. The only thing she ever asked me for was a CB. She wanted a CB, so I got her one. I got back from New Hampshire on Sunday and she told me, 'The antenna needs to be higher'". He laughs. "So I got the antenna mounted higher. She's been gone three years now." He looks at me, disbelief in his blue eyes. "When she got sick, she said, 'I don't want you to have to take care of me.' And I told her, 'You took care of me all those years, so now it's my turn.' And I did, till she died. She was a peach." Eyes behind heavy-rimmed glasses now fill with tears.

Talk then turns to work, of course, since most of the guests all work together at "the plant'. He brings out old pamphlets and booklets about his now-closed factory, telling his new boss, "I'll let you look at these, but you can't have 'em." The two men pore over the contents, our host pointing out products that he had helped make over time. "In September," he says, "I'll have been with Gorham for 43 years." A smile stretches his mouth. "Can you believe that?" He carefully folds the literature up and takes it back inside the mobile home.

Raindrops plop on the tent roof and make circles in the puddles in the street. A granddaughter wades, ankle deep, into the largest one. "Don't get wet," calls her granddad, laughing. People make ready to leave, 'before the rain gets any worse'.

"Don'cha wanna take some of these clams? They'll be good for lunch tomorrow." Deb comes to help. Father and daughter move as one, packing up clams and haddock for the guests. I look closely for The Peach, unseen, uncomplaining, and seem to see her there, in the closeness of the pair.

I'm Not a Real Doctor, But....

The doctor asked for the scalpel and cut a clean line from the collar bone to the sternum. *"Rib spreader"*, he barked.

"Rib spreader", Jo Don echoed. He sat in his scuffed, worn leather recliner and leaned forward raptly as Dr. Crawley reached into the chest cavity toward the torn aorta that he intended to repair. Joe Don held his breath. "He's using a 1.5 mil.Titanium glut. I wonder if that's going to give him enough room to move around the south ventricle."

Joe Don worriedly twisted his hands and gave his full attention to the operation now in full swing on *See it Now: Medical Update*. It was almost 11 p.m. and Dr. Crawley had to get this repair in hand, get the fifty-six year old man breathing on his own, plus cut to another commercial before the program ended in time for the 11 o'clock news. Joe Don found himself alternately holding his breath and expelling it carefully, his own hands moving as if he were slicing, stitching and repairing the delicate heart area instead of the TV doctors. His own heart was pounding with tension and concern for the doctor and the success of this procedure.

"Now, folks", Dr. Crawley's calm, gravelly voice cut through the silent operating theatre. *"We can all relax. The gentleman will be just fine. Dr. Stanhous, will you close for me? Just watch that little bleeder at 9 o'clock. It gave me a fit going in. You may have to reclamp it."* Dr. Crawley looked into the TV camera, his eyes friendly and reassuring over his surgical mask. *"Thanks for stopping in. Look in on us tomorrow when* Medical Update *will show the intricacies of surgery to relieve the pressure inside the brain. Until then, keep breathing!"* His eyes crinkled in a witty smile and he raised his bloody, gloved hand in farewell.

The screen cut to a series of commercials for yogurt, bran cereal and the benefits of fiber tablets. Joe Don sat back, his tension draining away. He didn't know why he got so uptight about Dr. Crawley's heart operations. He had complete faith in him and had never seen him goof up. I guess it's just the area, thought Jo Don. I mean, it is the *heart*-one slip and my God, you're gone! It's not like back surgery or even brain surgery, which might give you a little slack. But the *heart!* Jeez!

Joe Don flicked off the TV, stood up stiffly and ambled into the kitchen for a once-over of the refrigerator contents. Nothing looked appetizing so he reached for the plastic milk container, uncapped it and chugged at least two cups before replacing the cap and the container back on the shelf. He was careful to set the milk back behind the margarine tub so that his mom wouldn't suspect that he had had a gulp from the jug before hitting the sack. It was one of her pet peeves, his drinking from the container, and one that always brought on a tirade from his mother.

"You're just like your father, always drinking out of the jug!" she would rant. "And look where it got him. You'll go the same way, arteries clogged with fat and disease!" At which point Jo Don would always interject a blow-by-blow account of stent surgery (which he had seen Dr. Crawley perform many times). He would reassure her that at the first sign of any arterial blockage, he would go under the knife, get his stents, and return to her in full health. His mom never made it through all eight steps of the surgery before she threw up her hands and left the room. Joe Don knew this and added more details to the procedure each time he recounted it.

Joe Don made his way down the dark hall to his bedroom. He slept in the first bedroom to the left. His mom occupied the master bedroom at the back of the house. She rarely made it past 9:30 or 10 p.m. anymore. She usually dozed off in her flame-stitched wing back chair after *Hollywood Unfiltered* at eight o'clock. After that, Joe Don could be assured of having the TV to himself. He surfed through the cable stations listlessly until it was time for *Medical Update* at 10 p.m. Joe never missed a show. Over the years, Joe Don had watched Dr. Crawley and his handymen replace joints, set splintered tibias, heal the heart, lungs, spleen, and small intestines. While the men of medicine had worked, sawing and cutting, splicing and suturing, Joe Don himself had became a walking encyclopedia of medical terms, procedures, and jargon. He seemed to have a flair for processing medical terms and often quoted his heroes to his fellow workers, his mother, the barber, to anyone willing to list to the in-depth mysteries of hip replacement or heart by-pass. It was a standing joke at his workplace to "ask Dr. Joe Don if you're going in for surgery. He's not a real doctor but he'll know all about it!" Joe Don saw their teasing looks, but could never resist listing some dangers to look for with that particular type of surgery. Usually before he could finish his complete warnings, his co-workers would guffaw loudly, slap his shoulder and thank him for the "house call". Joe Don thought they meant well, but knew they didn't feel the devotion to the show that he did. He often felt that in a pinch, he could perform some of the *Update*'s procedures. HDTV provided great clarity. Now, he might need to handle all those instruments before starting in, but the actual procedures-piece of cake, thought Joe Don.

Joe Don yawned as he climbed into his bed and lay silently on his back for a few minutes. He was always tired after a *Medical Update* show, almost as tired as the doctors must feel after operating for hours at a time. Poor guys, they worked so hard, seeing patients, reading x-rays, and then performing their Olympian feats in the operating room each day. Joe Don often considered the limp, rather freakish looking lumps of flesh that lay on the tables awaiting the doctors' miracles, but his real empathy lay with the doctors, those godly figures in scrubs. Trim middle-aged men, often with graying temples, or balding heads, he loved the sound of their hushed voices explaining their procedures, their breath coming hard and noisily through their masks at times. *"Sutures, please, Ms. Haddon. Quickly! We don't want Mr. McMillan to wake up dead, now do we?"* Joe Don chuckled, thinking of Dr. Crawley's humorous comment on tonight's show. He flopped over to his left side (the best side for the blood's circulation at nighttime). That Dr. Crawley was something else. Not only the best surgeon, but a comedian to boot! Joe Don drifted quietly off to sleep.

Joe Don worked for City Showcase, a small but profitable furniture company on Route 11. He was one of the delivery men along with Frank Kisinsco, a tall, hard-muscled man of 50 with a beer gut that grew with the passing years. Joe loved Frank like a father. Joe Don's own father had died when Joe was 11 and Frank possessed many of the qualities that Joe Don remembered about his own dad. Frank liked his beer; so had Joe Don's dad. Frank loved wrestling and watched *WW Raw* every chance he got. Joe Don remembered his father staked out in front of the TV every Monday night while his mother loudly rattled the dishes in the kitchen to drown out the profanity, grunts, groans that accompanied the confrontations in the ring. The only difference in Frank and Joe Don's father was their efforts at conversation. Joe Don's father was a talker. A New Jersey man, words erupted out of him in quick, gunshot bursts. He was never silent. Frank, on the other hand, rarely said more than ten words a day to Joe Don. Joe didn't care. He filled their cab with medical stories from *Update* each afternoon and Frank listened carefully, adding a thoughtful grunt or a "You gotta be kiddin' me," if Joe Don got too graphic in his descriptions. Joe Don tried to keep his recounting simple for Frank. He knew the medical terms went right over Frank's head, and he had become expert in selecting just enough expertise and gory details to keep Frank on the edge of his seat. And it had paid off too. When Frank's mother had fallen and had to have her knee replaced, hadn't Joe Don told Frank to tell the doctor to check the circulation in her leg first before surgery? Turns out she was just like a case Dr. Crawley had treated in November. An old lady had to have angioplasty before she could get a knee replacement. Some sort of nerve damage from a previous surgery would have prevented the replacement from working. Frank's mother was fine today, walked to town once a day and tended her rose garden religiously. All thanks to Joe Don and of course, Dr. Crawley, Frank said. After that Frank usually stuck up for Joe when the other warehouse guys ribbed him about his "medical degree."

Today, Joe Don and Frank were on their way to Mrs. Cravitz's house on Plumtree Lane. She had finally made up her mind to purchase a rather hideous, (Joe Don thought), ornate reproduction piece for her foyer. It was a sort of hall tree-loveseat-hat rack thing, supposedly from the Jacobean period. Upholstered in red leather, its ornately carved wooden sides soared upward into gargoyles grimacing and grinning down from a height of six feet or more. It was a heavy piece of furniture, awkwardly loading into the van at the warehouse and Joe Don dreaded unloading the monster. Danny and Maury had used the forklift at the warehouse to help put it on the truck. Joe had asked Frank to get Danny to come with them, but Frank had said, "Nahh, we can handle it. Danny won't fit in the truck with us." Danny was a rather large guy who ate pizza for lunch each day and smelled heavily of garlic and Italian sausage for the rest of the afternoon. Joe had agreed and climbed into the cab with Frank driving. Frank always drove.

Mrs. Cravitz was waiting on the porch in front of her house, a little woman with graying hair tightly styled around her small face. Everything about Mrs. Cravitz was small except her house, her taste in furniture, and her glasses. She peered at the world through thick lenses that magnified her eyes eerily and completely covered her face from brow to lower cheek. The frames were heavy plastic tortoise shell. Attached to the glasses was a bright red woven cord that hung loosely down on both sides of Mrs. Cravitz's small head.

Frank and Joe got out of the van and approached Mrs. Cravitz's front steps. "Well, finally!" She spoke loudly for an older lady and peered down at them as they stood on the sidewalk below her. "I had just about given up on you! Well, just bring it in the front. It's going in the front hall." She moved quickly to open the front door, an orifice that Joe Don eyed skeptically. Mrs.

Cravitz's front entrance was prefaced with a flight of steep, narrow brick steps. It would be hell.

"Frank, I don't think that monster is going to go through there and besides that-those steps will be murder," he told his partner, quietly.

Frank frowned at the door with misgivings. It was an old one, narrow and tall to match the towering front wall of the house. "I don't think so either. Mrs. Cravitz", he called, "do you have a wider door in back? This fuck-er... er..piece of furniture isn't going to go in there."

Mrs, Cravitz turned to look at them, her eyes narrowing. "Well, I never! I think you just don't want to climb those stairs. Well, drive on in the back. You can come through the French doors off the patio. But I am warning you. I'm not moving *any* furniture out of your way." She entered the front door and closed it firmly. The men heard a distinct sound as a dead bolt lock slid into place.

"Old bat," muttered Frank. "You'd think she woulda thought of the size of that door before she bought this ugly piece a shit. Wadd'ya wanna bet? I bet we have to move all of her furniture before we can clear a path."

Joe Don climbed back into the cab. "I wonder if Mrs. Cravitz has ever thought about cataract surgery? You know, they do it with lasers now and it's real quick. Dr. Crawley's co-worker did three on one show last month. Those glasses of hers are way thick!"

Frank snorted. "Look, Joe, don't even go there. We're just here to move this monster inside. Concentrate on that. I don't need you drifting off into General Hospital and letting that one-ton bench drop on my foot or sumpin' worse." Frank drove the van slowly around back and pulled up to the stone patio. Joe Don observed the French doors just to the left of the patio and saw Mrs. Cravitz opening both doors wide.

"I love old doors like that, don't you, Frank? They look so British, or something," Joe Don sat quietly on the passenger's side while Frank irritably yanked the emergency brake back.

"British, huh? Tea and crumpets, that sort of thing?" Frank stepped out of the van and ambled to the back. Joe Don followed, glancing back at the French doors. He could just make out Mrs. Cravitz looking at them from outside the left door. She was leaning from side to side as if she thought they might just take off with her precious piece of furniture. Joe Don waved to her and wondered how well she could see him from her place on the patio. Lasers, he thought, I'll just mention them to her when we get finished. She's probably scared about the whole idea. Dr. Wang made it look easy that time and those people were reading the newspaper within days!

"Hurry up!" Mrs. Cravitz's voice ended Joe's medical thoughts. "I've got my air on. It doesn't come cheap, you know."

"Jesus Christ on a pony!" swore Frank from behind the hall tree in the van. "Has she actually looked at the size of this thing? It's not something you can carry with one hand. Joe, I'm going to ease this bitch forward. Now, you be careful. You're going to get the full weight before I can jump down there and help you. Since it's not boxed, be careful it doesn't hit the driveway. It may scratch and Old Man Vanceri will have our ass if we have to bring this mother back. Get ready!" Frank began to inch the monstrosity forward toward Joe who had braced himself for the full impact, his hands upraised.

Joe Don considered himself strong. He had lifted many sleeper sofas, the heaviest pieces of furniture on the market, and had carried many of them upstairs, with Frank on the other end. He always told his mother that he didn't need to work out. His job kept him in shape. But nothing had prepared him for the weight of this piece as it hurtled off the van and toward him. He caught it with his left hand low on one end. The piece shifted and pinned Jo Don's fingers under one of its legs against the driveway pavement.

"Oh, shit, Frank!" Joe Don screamed. The pain was unbearable. He would surely lose a finger.

Frank jumped down and knelt beside Joe Don. "Just relax, Joe. I'll lift it off ya'. Mother of God, this bitch is heavy—ummph!" Frank struggled and heaved upwards with a mighty grunt. The piece shifted enough for Joe Don to pull his hand out. He stared at his hand and gingerly flexed the fingers. That's what Dr. Crawley would have done to check for broken bones. Other than being red, swollen and skinned from the pavement, the fingers seemed okay. Skin was broken on the middle finger and Joe immediately stuck the finger in his mouth.

Frank frowned. "Is that the best thing, Doc? Dudn't look too hygienic to me."

Joe Don shook his head. "May not be, but it makes it feel better." He removed his finger and gave his hand a shake. "Thanks, Frank-I could have lost a finger. Whew! Well, let's get back to work. I can see Mrs. Cravitz is still worried about her open door."

"Fuck'er. Now, look, we're going to go slow. We've still got those patio steps to go up. I want you at the top this time. If there's any catching to do, I'll do it this time."

Frank and Joe Don began to wend their way across the remainder of the driveway, the stone patio, lifting the furniture, staggering a bit, slowly progressing toward the steps leading into the house. Both men paused when they reached the first step. The steps were also brick like those at the front of the house, but here, they were moss-covered, with ivy twining dangerously up the sides. Joe's heart sank at the sight of them.

"Did it rain out here this morning, Mrs. Cravitz? Those steps look pretty wet and slick." Joe Don turned to Mrs. Cravitz, as he wiped his sweaty forehead.

"Oh, for goodness' sakes! I watered my plants this morning. Those steps are perfectly fine. I wish you men would hurry up. My doors are wide open, letting in flies and letting out air!" Mrs. Cravitz came down the steps to glare up at both men, little fists curled into her hips.

"Come on, Joe," snarled Frank. "Let's get this over with." With a great effort, Joe Don lifted the hall-tree-coat rack-piece from hell, and Frank reciprocated with a mighty heave on his end. Together, they managed to waddle up four of the five steps. Mrs. Cravitz muttered something to herself that sounded a bit like "bunch of pussies", but Joe was breathing too hard to hear her well. *Mrs. Cravitz is wrong about these steps*, Joe Don thought. *They are squishy wet.* As he stepped backwards onto the last step, his heel caught. Startled, Joe lost his grip and watched in horror as the top heavy, gargoyle enriched thing seemed to topple slowly toward Frank. As Frank was knocked backward, the piece turned and pinned his neck under its ornate arm.

"Oh, my God, Frank!" Joe Don righted himself and struggled around the obstacle to look at his friend.

Frank was having trouble breathing, yet he was trying to push the thing off him with no success. Joe Don lifted fruitlessly on the opposite arm. *I've got to hurry*, he told himself. *Frank may d*...he was suddenly aware that Mrs. Cravitz had come to stand beside him.

"Mrs. Cravitz, call 911! Frank may have a crushed windpipe! I'm going to need help before the EMTs get here!" Joe knelt quickly beside Frank and reached into his pocket for his Swiss Army knife which he always kept handy for opening boxed furniture and removing tags from delivered furniture. Mrs. Cravitz turned toward the house. "Hurry, Mrs. Cravitz!" Joe shouted over his shoulder as he gently pressed on Frank's shoulder.

"Frank, I want you to keep calm. I can see you're having trouble breathing and I am going to cut into your windpipe to get you an airway going. Don't worry, I've seen Dr. Crawley do this several times. Just lay still."

Frank's eyes widened in horror as he continued to gasp for breath. He shook his head and tried to stay Joe Don's hand. Joe continued to lower the knife point to the hollow of Frank's neck. He plunged the point into the swollen, sweaty flesh. Frank's skin did not give and Joe Don pushed harder. *Jeez,* thought Joe Don. *I know what the rings of the trachea look like, but they are much deeper than I realized.* Joe pushed harder on the little blade. Blood oozed to the surface and then began to flow freely. Joe blinked. Blood was a lot redder than he thought and warm and it smelled. Joe gagged and dropped the knife, losing his breakfast in the wet ivy along the steps. He sat down on the wet steps and closed his eyes. He could hear Mrs. Cravitz grunting. Jo Don opened one eye carefully. What was Mrs. Cravitz doing to Frank? He watched through bleary eyes as Mrs. Cravitz used a shovel (where had that come from?) to lift the hall tree off of Frank's neck. Blood still oozed out of the hole in his neck and Joe quickly closed his eyes as his stomach heaved once more. *What is wrong with me?* he thought. *There was plenty of blood on Dr. Crawley's operating table and it never bothered me. But this...blood...smelled like metal and it was warm. And it was* Frank's!

Joe continued to sit on the wet step with his eyes closed until his head stopped whirling. Cautiously opening one eye, he saw Mrs.Cravitz swabbing Frank's neck and applying pressure to the area. The blood had slowed but Mrs. Cravitz was deftly replacing bloody gauze pads with thick clean ones.

"Mrs. Cravitz, I'm so sorry...I don't know what came over me. Is Frank....?"

"You lost it when you saw the blood, you silly nincompoop. Frank's going to be fine. EMTs will be here shortly. Nooo, now, you lie still, you old fart," she cautioned Frank, who was beginning to writhe under her administrations.

"Let me sit up," growled Frank, pushing her hand away.

"Can't do that, you may bleed out. Thank God, Dr. Kildare's knife wasn't sharp enough to go very deep or you might have been in real trouble," Mrs. Cravitz said as she carefully pushed Frank's beefy shoulders back down to the concrete.

Sirens could be heard down the street and grew louder as a First Responder van rolled into the driveway behind the delivery truck. Two EMTs parked the van and hopped out. Joe watched in awe as they rounded the truck with stretcher, oxygen tank and bags of equipment.

"Hey, Mrs. Cravitz, what'cha got here? Nothing you couldn't handle without us, I'll bet!" The taller of the two men grinned at Mrs. Cravitz. She grinned back and airily dismissed his praise.

"Well, I knew you guys needed some excitement this morning. These two nuts tried to kill each other bringing some furniture in my house. I've stopped the bleeding but you may need a steristrip on that cut." She sent Joe Don a ridiculing glance. "Swiss Army Knives can be dangerous in the wrong hands. And you might give this one some Finnigan if you have it. He seems to be a bit finicky at the sight of blood."

Joe Don struggled to his feet. "No, ma'am. I'm fine now. I was just worried about Frank and…"

"That's all right, young man. It takes some getting used to and if you know the patient, it's always harder," Mrs. Cravitz spoke in a softer tone as she let one EMT take her place at Frank's side. "Let's let Cal and Lester do their magic and you and I will get a nice cup of coffee, hmm? Might even have a shot of something stronger to get you back on your feet."

Two weeks later, Frank and Joe Don were wending their way out I36 to the community of Wayfare. Today they were delivering some nursery furniture to a young couple expecting their first baby. Frank was in a fine mood, humming an old Frank Sinatra tune in a burbling tone

"Hey, Joe Don," rasped Frank. His throat had healed well but the pressure of the hall tree had left bruising and trauma to his larynx.

Joe Don turned toward his partner. I'm so glad he didn't die, thought Joe. "Yeah, Frank?"

Frank leaned toward Joe Don with a half smile on his lips. "Guess where I went last night?"

"Don't know. Bowling? Tuesday's bowling, isn't it?

Frank laughed. "No, not even close! I went over to Rose's house. We watched *911 Marathon*. You know, those shows about EMTs and their routines. They are something else. Just like Cal and Lester and Rose, of course, helped me, these guys and gals are really smart!"

Joe Don was puzzled. "Who's Rose?"

Frank looked at Joe Don in amazement. "Mrs. Cravitz! Mrs. Rose Cravitz. She taught emergency procedures and trained EMTs for years at the community college. She even trained Cal and Lester. I tell you, if it hadn't been for them, I'd a died right there in her driveway."

"Frank, I'm sorry about that day. I guess I had watched too much *Medical Updates*. I really thought I could help you." Joe Don cringed every time he thought about that morning.

"Naah! Don't worry about it. It's just a good thing Rose was our customer. She's really a sweetheart. She explains procedures to me when we watch *911 Marathon*. She makes it so clear that I think maybe I could help somebody. I know I could operate the defibrillator and using the paddles to restart the heart, a piece of ca....!

"Hold it right there, Frank! Don't say another word! Don't try those things. That's what got me in trouble," interrupted Joe Don.

"Yeah, but it looks so easy on TV and Rose would help me, I'm sure. You know, she and I have a thing going on. We're together a lot. And to think we'd never have met without that god awful piece of furniture! It was just meant to be...." Frank yammered on and on. Joe Don longed for the old silent Frank.

In fact, Joe Don had become the silent one as Frank seemed to replace Joe Don in the description department. Now, folks at worked rolled their eyes behind Frank's back as he held forth on emergency tactics and his admiration of Rose. Well, he for one would never ever run his mouth about a TV show again. The thought of watching Dr. Crawley and his team again made Joe Don shudder. He had switched to HGTV. Boy, those makeover shows were something else. Joe really liked the ones that redid the kitchens. His mom had been talking about updating her kitchen and he thought if he had the right kind of tools, he just might be able to do that by himself and save her a lot of money. Last night, the crew of *Phoenix from the Ashes* took down an interior wall in about three seconds. Joe had gotten really nervous when the sledge hammer came too close to a load-bearing beam, but those guys knew exactly what they were doing.

"I wonder what a sledge hammer would cost," Joe mused out loud. He glanced at Frank who shot him a baffled look.

"What the hell do you need with a sledge hammer, Joe?"

"Well, it's the best thing for tearing down interior walls, Frank. And it really looks like fun! You see, I was watching this show last night. It's called *Phoenix from the Ashes* and these guys really brought the house down! Literally! You see, they start with a basic layout of the original room and then...."

Frank cleared his throat noisily and sent a threatening look at his young partner. Joe, who was watching the road, sped up the idolatry of his new TV heroes. Frank began to hum Sinatra louder and louder, the van rolling on down toward Wayfare.

Queen of Puppy Feet

Martha had called Caroline at school to come home. Her daddy was giving her a fit, she said. Caroline asked Martha to stay with her father for a couple of hours so she could leave during her planning period to see what was going on, but Martha wouldn't listen. Caroline stood in the main office, worriedly twisting a strand of blond hair.

"Caroline, he's too much for me today. I can't take another minute. You come on home. He'll be better when you get here-he always is," Martha spoke in a loud, forceful voice. Caroline sighed and hung up the phone. She turned to face Shirley Dunford, the school secretary. Shirley scared Caroline to death.

"Shirley, can you watch my class until the bell rings. I can't stay...my father..." Caroline stumbled to a halt when she looked at Shirley's stern face. Shirley was the secretary who called the substitutes each morning. Caroline thought that by that look on Shirley's face that she was probably not going to get many calls next week, but what could she do? Her daddy shouldn't be left alone.

"I'll come on down there in a few minutes. You going to get somebody for the other two periods? You might ask Coach Starnes. He doesn't have any more classes today," Shirley spoke in a clipped tone.

"Yes, that's what I'll do. I'll call him on the intercom. It'll save time," said Caroline. Starnes owed her a couple of favors anyway. She had kept his Basketball Fundamentals class three times last week.

Caroline left the school a half hour later and drove carefully down Main Street and out onto Harding Street toward her father's two story house on Maple Avenue. The house stood, as she had always known it, nestled between the junipers that lined the sides and front of the house. When she was little, she always thought of the bushy, fragrant trees as little sentinels guarding her house. Nowadays, the trees were looking shabby like old men who badly needed haircuts. Well, she thought as she drove into the driveway, at least they hide the peeling paint. As she got out of the car, she wondered again what her father had done to upset Martha so much that she had called her to come home. That mystery was soon solved when she lifted her eyes and beheld her father coming toward her.

Her father was walking resolutely down the front walk, pajama shirt opened at the top, fleece-lined slippers flapping on his slew feet, and his naked rear and privates shining for all the world to see.

"Poppy, what are you doing out here? Where are your pants? Where's Martha?" She got her father by the arm and guided him toward the house.

From the front door, Martha was yelling at the top of her lungs. "Caroline, I told him to stay put. He done peed his pants again with me packed and ready to go home. Bring him on back up here. I got him some clean pants to put on."

With his daughter beside him, Myron walked jauntily into the living room. Caroline deposited him rather dispiritedly on the sofa and he had a good look down at his wrinkled and graying pubic area. "What is all this?" he demanded. "What have you done with my pants? You two...wenches! Where are my britches?" He began to breathe heavily, feeling violated and exposed to the four eyes turned on him.

"Here are your pants. Let me help you put them on," offered Caroline, holding the flannel pajamas out to him as she took his right arm to help him off the sofa.

"Leave me alone, I can put my own pants on! Haven't I been doing it all my life?" Myron snorted and stood shakily, grabbing the pajamas from his daughter and tottering on one foot.

"Easy," cautioned Caroline. "Martha, you go on home. We'll be fine. Poppa just forgot what he was doing. He's never had this problem before. We'll talk a little later. Maybe eating supper will straighten him up. You go on, now. I don't know if they will call me Monday. Marion's supposed to be back Monday. Can I call you to come stay with him, if they need me?"

Martha shook her head. "No, I got to keep my grandchildren next week, Caroline."

Caroline nodded. She understood. Martha was not ready to take care of an old man's incontinence, but was she? She walked to the front door behind Martha who was gathering up her things in a hurry. "Thanks, Martha. I'll have you a check ready on Monday." Martha grunted and went heavily out to her car which she started with a roar.

Myron had followed Caroline to the door and watched Martha leave with great interest. "Damn, they's in a hurry. Who was that, Caroline?"

"Oh, Pa, you know it was Martha leaving," Caroline answered tiredly. "Can't you remember anything?"

"Oh, I remember a lot of things. I'm going fishing! I caught me some lizards and they're in a coffee can out back. I'm going in the morning."

"Well, that's just fine, but let's have dinner now. What did Martha start for us, do you know, did you watch her?" Caroline began rummaging in the refrigerator finding tuna, a plate of tomatoes and cukes, and a bowl of lima beans. She set these out on the table.

"Seems like she was making cornbread muffins. I smelled 'em in the pan, like your mama used to make 'em with cracklin's in the bottom of the pan. Mmmm! I hope that's what we're having, with a big ol' pot of brown beans. Let's go eat, I'm pretty hungry, after chasing them little lizards all afternoon."

Caroline began to set plates around the old enamel topped table in the kitchen and put the teapot on to boil. Her father seated himself at the table in the place he had occupied since Caroline had known him and proceeded to help himself to tomatoes and cucumbers. His false teeth snapped loosely and sloppily up and down, up and down, on the vegetables until he worked up a fine mess of drool down his chin. Caroline used a paper towel to wipe her father's face, but he pushed her impatiently away. "Where's that cornbread, Caroline, I can wipe my own face."

"Poppy, there's only tuna and limas tonight. How about a nice tuna sandwich?" She knew how this would be answered before the words were out of her mouth.

"Tuna? No, I want cornbread. Can't I ever have what I want? It's my house! And I want some cornbread muffins. Now!" Myron's heavy fist pounded the table, causing the silverware to bounce and slide across the surface. Caroline caught her fork before it hit the floor and then placed her hand on her father's closed fist.

"Pa, stop it. I don't have time to fix cornbread. Now, you'll have to eat your supper. If you do, we'll play a game of Rummy before I do the dishes. Okay? Would you like that?" She looked into his face which so much resembled a stubborn four-year old more so than a 74-year old and saw it soften at the mention of the favorite game.

"Well, I'll whip your ass at rummy, young lady. You don't ever beat me at Rummy," Myron said slyly, forking his tuna into his mouth. "No one beats me at Rummy." Caroline smiled just as slyly back at her daddy. Maybe not, but I beat you at the dinner game, she thought to herself.

He settled himself back in his kitchen chair with his favorite deck of cards after she had cleared away their dishes, and Caroline thought, as she had many times, how strange old age was. How could her father's thoughts and memories of two minutes before be zapped from his brain, but he could remember the rules of a beloved card game and continue to play it rather well?

"Which way do you want the discard stack to run-toward you or me?" he asked, intently dealing the cards across to her.

"Point them toward you. I won't be using them much. I'm going to whip you with what you deal me. You can have my discards," Caroline grinned maliciously at her old daddy.

"Bullshit," he answered, his face taking on a determined, and younger look. "Here we go, little girl. Get ready to lose your ass."

Cards were played, discarded, spreads laid, points made and lost. Caroline was holding out for a third ace from the deck to match the two in her hand when her father chuckled loudly as he picked up the discard pile about six deep. "Watch this, smartie," he crowed, as he laid down a run of five clubs beginning with the nine. His hand shook as he fanned them out for her to see. This play was followed by three deuces and a five on her spread of fives. "And I'm out! Count up my points, Caroline, didn't I whip you? That puts me over 500, I betcha!"

Caroline smiled and began to gather her father's spreads. She counted aloud so he could hear the point values. "Five, ten, twenty-five, sixty-five.... Yep, you are well over 500, Pa. You beat me for sure..." She stopped counting as her father snatched up the queen of clubs from the counted cards.

"You didn't count her! The queen of....of..." Myron groped for the suit name. "Those little things... queen of...of puppy feet!" He christened the lady loudly. "The queen of puppy feet, you didn't count her. She's worth ten points!"

Caroline laughed. "Queen of puppy feet. How did you come up with that, Pa? She's the queen of clubs! And I did so count her!"

Her father was studying the queen's face interestedly. "The sign looks like a puppy foot, you know a paw print?" Caroline watched her father's face as he looked intently at the card. Well, it does, she had to agree. Clever old thing. How hard it must be for old, familiar words to fail you, she thought. Think of all the words we waste in our life and how valuable they all become at the end of our lives. She was thinking of the teenagers she dealt with at the high school and their constant, seemingly meaningless chatter.

Her father was still holding the card tightly in his hand. "Let me have the card, Pa. We've got to get ready for bed. You have to have your bath," Caroline held out her hand for the card.

"No, I want to look at her. She looks...like...your mother...No, no, not her. She seems to favor...Caroline! Caroline, look, it's you. It's your picture! See how her eyes look?" Myron held the card out excitedly for her to see the likeness. "Look, it's you, it's Caroline."

Caroline looked at the queen's unsmiling, rather tired-looking face and laughed. "Well, she looks tired like me, that's for sure, but it's not me, Daddy, it's the queen of clubs. Not me."

Her father stubbornly shook his head. "No, no, no, it's not...she's queen of puppy feet, like I said. And it is your picture. You're wearing that little vest that your momma made for you for your first grade picture. Remember the one that had all that color in it? She loved that vest. You didn't like it, remember, said it made you look like a hinkle!" The old man snorted. "A hinkle. That was your grandma's word and you picked it up. Used to make your mom and me laugh to hear you say it. Well, there it is, in full color, you in your vest, all dressed up for first grade pictures, Miss Queen." He handed her the card and looked at her, his face full of memories and love for that long ago child.

Caroline studied her father's face, looking for that witty, fast-thinking man that had been her father. Where had he gone? He appeared from time to time, to play cards, to read the newspaper some days, or to tell Caroline what vegetables to plant in March and which ones to plant in May. There was still plenty of smarts in that old head, but when it chose to show itself was becoming less and less.

"Poppy, what do you think the Queen is going to do with you? The Queen needs to work as many days as she can. I can't stay home with you and have enough money to feed us and keep up this house. Do you know what you did today to make Martha so angry?" Caroline had reached out to hold her father's hand. His hand and long tapering fingers were soft, with a dry, hot feel as if the old man had a temperature.

"I don't know no Martha. Who's she? Was she here today? Wasn't she that woman that used to help your mama with the apple butter?" Myron queried, removing his hand from Caroline's. He rubbed his forehead worriedly. "Why are you mad at me, Caroline? I didn't do anything. Are you mad because I said you looked like that...that ...queen? I didn't mean to hurt your feelings. You're my purty girl, you know that." Myron looked at Caroline sorrowfully.

Caroline had to laugh. "No, Poppy, I'm not mad at that. In fact, I like being a queen. And looking like one is even better. I'm just worried about you. You wet your pants today. That hasn't happened before. It upset Martha.

Do you remember doing that? Were you trying to get to the bathroom when it happened? Can you tell me about it?"

Her father frowned as he seemed to search his mind. He shook his head slowly. "I can't remember going to the bathroom at all today." He brightened all of a sudden. "I do remember wading in the stream out back of Old Man Harry's house. I was looking for bluegills. They'll come right up to your feet, you know, Caroline, and bite the immortal hell out of you if they are hungry enough. That water was always so cold."

Caroline listened to her father and then heard a dribbling, puddling sound. She jumped to her feet.

"Oh, shit, Pop! You've done it again! You peed your pants!" She ran to get a towel from the bathroom as Myron struggled to his feet.

"Hell! I'm sorry, Caroline. I thought I was in the water...I...I'll help, bring me a towel," Myron looked embarrassedly as his daughter began to dab at his legs and the warm puddle at his feet.

"No, I'll get this, Poppy. Don't worry about it. That's what happened to you and Martha today, do you remember now? Maybe you were thinking about fishing or wading and you just went," Caroline suggested. She got her father's arm and led him toward the bathroom. "Can you go in there and get ready for your bath? The Queen of Puppy Feet has had it with this puppy and his puddles!" She laughed lightly, hoping he would get her joke. He chuckled. Caroline really felt like crying.

"Yes, Queen, your Majesty," Myron shuffled into the bathroom and shut the door.

For the rest of the evening Caroline was the "Queen of Puppy Feet" to her father. She used it to its full advantage, getting her father to make sure he went to the bathroom before he got in bed because the Queen ordered it, and to go to sleep quickly because the Queen had other people to tend to. Her father giggled and obeyed his Queen's wishes, snuggling down into his pillow, his teeth in an Efferdent bath for the night. He smiled up at her, as toothless and as beguiling as a baby.

"Goodnight, Queen of Puppy Feet," he whispered.

"Goodnight, o faithful subject. Sleep well," answered the fair queen, folding the quilt back under her father's arm and patting his shoulder. She hoped this would be a peaceful night and the old man wouldn't get up to wander the house as he sometimes did. Once, she had found him at three a.m. cooking potatoes, the stove eye dangerously hot.

Later, in front to the TV, Caroline pondered this new problem with caring for her father. Until now, a sitter for the day while she worked a few days a week had been the best answer. Her father's biggest problems had been forgetfulness and a tendency to talk about the past and people long dead. He would wander off if no one was with him, but he ate well, seemed to digest his food fine, and until today, bathroom issues had not been of any concern. What could she do? A rest home was out of the question. There was no money for such a thing; she needed to go back to teaching full time in order to have some money for that. Day care for an old man was as expensive as for toddlers, she had found out. And now after today's wet pants, Martha wouldn't be back, Caroline knew that. Who would watch him when the school called again? If she turned them down many times, they would just find someone else. Caroline's head began to ache. Must be the weight of my crown, she told herself, ruefully. The Queen of Puppy Feet has had some heavy issues today.

"Well, Queen?" Caroline lifted her glass of ginger ale. "What does your cabinet of ministers think? What does the royal soothsayer say? Your ladies-in-waiting? Your gentleman of the bedchamber?" Caroline giggled. "No, wait a minute. You can't have one of those. They were for the king. You would have had a lady of the bedchamber. I don't even have a man for the bedchamber, much less a gentleman or lady! Oh, lackaday, wella wella! Woe is me," Caroline smirked and drained her glass. "It's late. I'm going to bed."

One by one, the Queen of Puppy Feet turned out the lights of her kingdom and found her way upstairs to the small bathroom that her parents had proudly built years ago—"Just for you, Caroline," her father had told her then. As Caroline brushed her teeth, she surveyed herself in the mirror. I don't know what to do, she told her reflection. When I left Bobby Ray and came back home, I was the one needing help. Now it's Poppy in need of parenting and I have no idea how to be a parent.

She had a moment picturing herself as a young mother, something that would most likely never happen now. She stared at her reflection. I need a haircut, she thought. And maybe some highlights for the winter. She clicked off the light and went to the bedroom she had had as a child.

From her bedroom window, the street light cast an orangish glow on to the front lawn. The lawn will need mowing at least once more, Caroline told herself. Then fall leaves to pick up. She shuddered. She had always hated yard work but since she had moved back home, she had taken over all these tasks.

Her dad certainly couldn't help although he was full of advice about how to mow, rake and fertilize.

She got into bed and lay on her back. *Maybe the sandman will bring me an answer,* remembering that old song her mom used to sing. *'Mr. Sandman, bring me a dream. Make him the cutest I've ever seen.'* Now that wouldn't be a bad idea! Caroline grinned, yawned and wearily closed her eyes.

"Caroline! Caroline!" Myron yelled up the stairs where Caroline was getting dressed. "Where's my damn lizards? I left 'em on the back porch and now they're gone. Even the can's gone. If that damn cat of yours has been in there again, I'll wring its goddamn neck!"

Caroline peered down the steps at her angry father as he clutched the banister with one hand and shook his free fist in the air. "Calm down, Pa. I'll be down in a second. Let me get my shoes on." Caroline went back to her room and took her time looking for her New Balance tennis shoes. "Let him stew awhile," she told herself. "Maybe he'll forget about them. I've got too much to do today to mess with a bunch of nonexistent lizards."

When Caroline came down stairs about ten minutes later, she found her father sitting at the kitchen table, his long fingers laced together, the index finger of his right hand thumping up and down on between the first two fingers of his left hand, a sure sign of impatience and further evidence that he hadn't forgotten his lost lizards.

"Well, Caroline, where are they? Did you throw them out last night after I went to bed? You know I was going fishing today!"

"Poppy, I didn't touch your lizards. I want you to calm down and think, real hard. Did you really catch lizards yesterday or did you just imagine it in your mind, like last week when you thought you saw Mama in the back yard hanging up clothes? You know, that seemed real to you, too, just like catching lizards."

Her father's eyes blinked rapidly as if he were trying not to cry. He looked bewildered and as lost as any child who had had a dream explained away. "No, I wasn't imaginin' 'em. I caught 'em, all of 'em, and put 'em in my coffee can. They was right out there on your mama's freezer, waiting for me...I...I could feel 'em, all cold and squiggly....I...think I caught 'em". Myron shook his head in frustration. "Oh, shit, I'm not sure of anything anymore." Elbows on knees, his long hands opened to receive his graying, balding head.

"Pa, don't feel too bad. It's probably too windy to fish anyway," Caroline countered. "Besides, I need you to help me today. Do you want to go to

33

Modern-Mart with me? We need some groceries and I have got to buy some underwear. My panties have no more elastic and I would hate to lose a pair in front of those evil ninth graders of Mrs. Turner's." She laughed hoping to get a corresponding chuckle from her father. Instead, he raised an angry face, eyes red-rimmed and furious.

"Hell, no, I'm not going to Modern-Mart. Goddamned Communists! I hate settin' foot in that store and I'd just as soon not have you traipsin' in there every time the door opens, either, missy!" Myron raised his head from his hands to glare at his daughter. His eyes just looked angry now, not full of confusion and self-pity as before.

"Well, in that case, stay here, because I have got to go this morning and see what the Communists have to sell. Will you promise to stay in the house? You can watch Courthouse Justice at 10 o'clock and Judge Karen comes on Channel 11 after that." Myron loved the TV court shows and would sit enraptured, happy to cuss the plaintiffs, defendants, and judges alike as "a pack of idiots". Justice never seemed to take place to Myron's way of thinking, but he enjoyed the shows each day. Caroline could usually leave him from ten o'clock to twelve to run errands without having to worry about him too much. After yesterday's bathroom accidents though, she wondered if she could continue to have this respite. If he makes a mess, I'll just clean it up, she told herself.

She turned on the TV as Myron settled into his recliner behind her. She brought him a second cup of coffee from the kitchen and ran back upstairs to get a jacket. When she came down, Myron had left his chair and was nowhere to be found in the house.

"Poppy! Poppy!" Caroline called, as she checked the bathroom, spare bedroom and small den off of Myron's bedroom. "Where in the shit did he go to? Old man, if he was in the grocery store with me, I couldn't move slow enough for him, but let him get a wild hair and he's gone like Snyder's Hound."

She glanced out the front door and spied her father sitting in the front seat of the car, on the passenger's side, and looking impatiently at his watch. Sighing loudly, she gathered her purse and keys and went out, locking the door behind her. She slid into the driver's seat and fixed her father with an exasperated stare.

"Well, what changed your mind about the Communists?"

"I remembered that I needed to get some Milk of Magnesia. You'd forget to get it."

"I could remember Milk of Mag, Pop. I get it every time you tell me to."

"No, I'll go in. I want to see who the Greeter is this week. Might be Minnie Hawkins," her father winked knowingly at Caroline. "You know how she likes to flirt with me."

"All right, you can go, but I want you to tell me if you have to go to the bathroom. Do you remember what happened yesterday? I don't want to ride around town with an old man with wet britches."

"Aghh!" Myron waved his hand impatiently in the air. "Don't worry about that, Caroline. I remember what happened. I'll let you know, now, let's go." Caroline started the car.

Modern-Mart was jammed with cars and customers. It was always like this on Saturday morning and Caroline wondered what had possessed her to pick this day to shop. And to make matters worse, once in the parking lot, Myron refused to get out of the car.

"Come on, Pop. What about Minnie? Don't you want to see her? You said you did," urged Caroline, afraid of leaving him alone in the car. She knew he wouldn't stay put and there was that possibility now of the bladder problem.

"Minnie who? I don't know no Minnie. Let me sit here. It's warm in here and I'm sleepy!" Myron drew up his shoulders and crossed his arms. "I'll be all right in the car. Lock me in!"

Caroline got out of the car, exasperated. "Now, stay here. I'm not going to be back in a minute. If you get tired of waiting, come in the store and have Customer Service page me. Pa, promise you won't wander off. That could be dangerous." She stooped to gaze pleadingly at her father.

"Oh, go on. I'll be fine," he dismissed her with another impatient wave of his hand.

Caroline slammed the door and locked the car with her key. Maybe he *would* think he was locked in. God, I don't care anymore, she thought. Let him wander off into traffic. I've lost my patience.

She walked quickly through the automatic doors. Once inside the "Community Bulletin Board" struck her eye and she stopped to read the notices about yard sales, fish fries, and church bake sales that were always going on in the community.

Hmm, Seventh Day Adventists are having a bake sale—I might stop by there and get an apple pie. Mrs. Watson makes the best ones at that church, Caroline mused to herself. Ooh, an estate auction. Old Mr. Collins' place is finally ready. I guess the children have gone through what they wanted. Let's see...jewelry, wardrobes, kitchen appliances, outdoor furniture. I might go after I finish here. Poppy might enjoy it and we can get a hot dog. Harold's secretary will be fixing hot dogs, I'm sure. The auction, she had already noticed, was being conducted by Harold Weiss, a local auctioneer and real estate man and one of Caroline's high school classmates. Harold had gone into business with his father right after high school, learned the rudiments of the auctioneer's trade, and now conducted most of the old man's business. He was known for his fairness in business and his rhythmic auctioneer chants. He held the esteemed title of "Grand Auctioneer of the Ninth District", and Caroline, for one, was very proud that one of her classmates had done well for himself. Yes, an auction would be a good way to spend the rest of the morning. It might tire her dad out and he would take a good nap. She hoped he had given up all ideas of fishing.

Held up by the multitude of shoppers and precious few check out cashiers, Caroline found herself worrying about her father being alone for so long in the car. Why didn't I make him come inside? Or make him stay at home? She knew the answer to both those questions. Myron did what he wanted to do.

Once outside, she quickly glanced over the parking lot. No old man or ambulances appeared and she hurriedly pushed her buggy toward the gray Olds that was her dad's old car. "Old Betsy", Myron called her affectionately. Lo and behold, her father was still perched upright in the car, although he seemed a bit impatient with her when she stored her bags in the trunk and slipped back into the car. He had rolled down his window and had hung his arm out over the window sill. She sniffed the air suspiciously as she slid into her seat. Nothing, she thought, just old man sweat. Good enough.

"Well, it took you long enough. I thought I'd suffocate in here," he complained, as she got her keys out. Caroline turned to look her father over closely. Besides a mild sheen of perspiration on his forehead, he seemed to be fine, certainly not dehydrated, and in fact, she thought he looked rested, as if he had napped while she was in the store.

"Well, Pop, you could have come with me. I would have put you in one of those electric carts and you could have run all over the store, but you wouldn't go in. Besides, I'll bet you had a good nap."

"Did not! I had a visitor, couldn't nap. Bobby Ray stopped by and we had a good talk."

Caroline had put the car into reverse and had begun to back out of her space, but she slammed her foot on the brake, throwing her father and herself forward against the seatbelts. She turned a flushed face to Myron.

"Bobby Ray was here? What did you talk about? What did he want?"

"He didn't want nothin'. Just saw me sitting here, burnin' up and stayed to chat awhile. I always liked Bobby Ray. Don't know why you left him," Myron glanced at Caroline out of the corner of his eye. She glared at her father and then shifted her gaze back over her shoulder and continued to back up the car.

"Yeah, well, I had my reasons which I'd rather not go into right now while I'm driving. Pop, we're going to an auction. Weiss's has Mr. Jasper Collins' place up for auction this morning. Let's go see what they have and we can get a hot dog. You like Harold's hot dogs, don't you? Can you wait to go to the bathroom out there? I'll get Harold to let us go in the house. I know you don't like Port-a-Potties."

"Hmph! I've already gone, thank you. I went in Modern-Mart and used their facilities. You were gone so long, I thought I would pop. Had me a Coke with Minnie, too, while I was there. And some chips!" Myron looked triumphantly at his daughter as she eased the car out of the parking lot and back on to Route 8 which would take them on out to the Collins farm. She hoped that this would distract her father away from the topic of Bobby Ray. That was a subject she didn't even want to think about today.

Caroline blinked rapidly a few times and refocused on her driving. She began to relax as the town gave way to green fields and black angus cattle grazing contentedly.

"Cows are soothing to watch, aren't they, Pop?" Caroline mused.

Her father grunted, "Yeh, as long as I don't have to feed'em or chase 'em down." Myron pulled his ball cap further down on his forehead and seemed to doze off.

Caroline saw the auction signs right before the Collins' driveway. Cars lined the drive way and Harold has some teenagers parking cars in the grassy area in front of the house. "We're here, Poppy," she announced to her father, who sat up, blinking himself awake. "I'm about ready for that hot dog, aren't you?"

"Yep, I am. He will have some coffee, won't he? He used to fix a big silver pot of coffee at his sales," said Myron, stirring in his seat. "I really could use a cup of coffee."

"I'm sure that there will be coffee of some kind there. You don't think I would have brought you out here without some coffee being offered do you?" Caroline teased. Myron's love of coffee was well-known. Millions of cups he had consumed in his life and always kept the rest of the morning's brew in an old-fashioned glass lined thermos in order to "have something to sip on" during the day.

The auction crowd was making its rounds of the merchandise when Caroline and her father drove up. Most of Jasper Collins' household furniture and kitchen goods were sitting outside his house for display before the auction. Like most auctioneers, Weiss found that things went faster when folks had a chance to look over the big items before bidding. Even if his customers didn't know the difference in cane-bottomed chairs and burled veneers, they seemed to appreciate being able to check things out before the bidding began. Caroline opened the door for her father and looked around for the aluminum-folding table where hot dogs and drinks were being sold.

"Let's get our hot dog, Pop, and then we can go around and look at stuff. I want to check out the lawn furniture. It might be in good shape and we could use some chairs for summer." Caroline headed her father in the direction of the food table. There were a few chairs around the table and Caroline thought that she might leave her father there to finish his hot dog and coffee while she wandered around the sale items. If he could get refills on his coffee, he would be happy for awhile. If he got too tired, they could always go home.

"Let's sit here, Poppy, until the auction starts," Caroline directed, pulling out two chairs for them. Her dad plopped down and immediately began looking for his promised coffee.

"Where's that coffee and hot dog, Caroline? I'm hungry enough to eat two of 'em."

"Just a sec...Diane, give me three dogs and a coffee." Caroline handed a ten to Diane Phlegar, Harold's secretary and Gal Friday. She always made up the hot dogs before the auctions and packed them in a large cooler. Coffee was poured piping hot from the big silver urn well known to Weiss's customers.

Diane handed Caroline the dogs and coffee with a wink. "Mr. Arrowood, you're looking right pert this morning. It's good to see you two, Caroline."

"You, too, Diane. Listen can you keep an eye on my dad for a few minutes? I want to look at the lawn furniture. Just keep his cup full."

"Sure will, hon. He can tell me what he thinks of my coffee!"

Caroline laughed. "No doubt he'll tell you how to make it. Thanks, Diane. I won't be long."

When the auction started, Caroline found a place near the front and took a seat. She looked for her father at the food table but he was nowhere to be seen. Should she go looking for him? Probably not. He knew where the car was and lots of people here knew Myron. They would come get her if he seemed addled. She could only hope that he wouldn't need the bathroom, although with his coffee drinking, it was probably a reason to hunt him down.

Her concern ended with Harold Weiss's loud greeting of "Mornin', neighbors. Glad you could come out. We hope that we'll have few things that you might want this morning. Mr. Collins's family wants to thank you all for coming and wants you to know that any goods that you buy today will be most appreciated. You all remember Sandy and Gail. They live up in Raleigh now and would like to wrap up their daddy's estate as soon as possible. So, let's get started with Number One, that old walnut bureau. Now you may be interested in knowing that this bureau came from England with the Collins family way back in 1815. It's solid black walnut with cut glass pulls and it's in pretty good condition. Let's start off with a bid of $425, now who'll give me 500...550..600..I hear 625...25....25...25...let's have a 650....50....come on folks, all the way from England! You don't see wood like this nowadays.... who'll say 645....45....45."

Harold's voice drew Caroline in with its quick chanting melody. Harold had a way of starting out strong and then he would begin to plead, offering to throw in some old worthless trinket or hauling home the piece of furniture himself for the new owner. His audience loved his banter and often threw out comments questioning the value of the item or sometimes, Harold's sanity over certain prices. Harold deftly handled all comments and kept up his steady chant. His assistants kept track of the bidders cards and offerings. Caroline found herself highly entertained by Harold's voice. It was hypnotic and well, almost sexy, the way he strutted across his platform, stopping to throw a fist into the air, or extend an open palm at a hesitant customer with a questioning expression on his face. She was having a good time and didn't even mind when the lawn furniture was bought by her neighbor, Mr. Coker. It was fun, bidding, though. She had her limit of $100 and when Coker offered $120, she gladly bowed out. Harold announced, "That's all right, Caroline! I'll bring over a chair this summer and we'll go visit Coker for some lemonade! That okay with you, Coker? I mean, you owe her. She wanted that furniture bad!"

Everyone laughed as Mr. Coker agreed to serve lemonade if Harold brought the lemons. Caroline laughed with the crowd and gave Harold a friendly wave.

The items to be auctioned from the house were dwindling and Caroline got up to find her father, a task that took her a good twenty minutes. She could hear Harold's chanting and bidding shouts from the crowd as she wandered out to the barn in search of Myron.

"Dad? Are you out here?" she called before stepping into the cool darkness of the old barn. Inside there were stalls for cows long dead. The sweet dusty smell of hay and straw was still redolent in the air and Caroline suddenly remembered coming here with her father years ago to buy freshly churned butter from Mr. Collins and his wife. Mrs. Collins used a butter press with a flower design to make her blocks of butter. She could still feel the greasy waxed paper that Mrs. Collins used to wrap up her butter. It rode in Caroline's lap on the way home in a brown paper bag, the sides splotched with greasy spots. Her father thought there was nothing better than the Collins' butter. All gone, Caroline thought. No one to make butter now, or any desire to do so. It was sad to see these old homes and way of life die. There was no need for them, but something was being lost that wouldn't be replaced, Caroline knew.

Caroline made her way back to the car in hopes of finding her father there and sure enough, there he stood, leaning against the car, as if he had been waiting for her.

"Poppy, where in the world have you been?" asked Caroline. "Are you worn out? I got into the auction and left you on your own. Do you want to find a bathroom? Where were you?"

"At the auction, o'course! I bought something!" Myron announced proudly. "Wait'll you see!"

Caroline stopped and looked her father in the eye. "Pop, what did you buy? I didn't know you had any money. What is it? Oh, Pop, I hope you didn't buy an animal! Tell me you didn't buy a horse or a buggy to put in the yard! Did you buy that old wardrobe? Poppy, that thing weighs a ton. We don't have any place to put it!" Caroline began to fret, imagining a huge loss of income, plus her father's determination to bring home whatever he had bought.

"Oh, hush, silly! I bought a cider mill and the chopper that goes with it. They came at a good price. Harold's bringin' 'em over Monday morning. Damn cider mill looks almost brand new. Jasper must not have known what he was doing with the thing." Myron opened up the car door and sat heavily in the seat. "Whew, Caroline, come on, I'm tired. Let's go home."

Caroline walked around the car, got in and faced her father. "A cider mill, Dad? Why didn't you just buy a still?"

Myron grinned. "Jasper didn't have one, or I might've. Come on, let's go. I can't wait to have some cider."

Caroline was up by 7 a.m. on Monday morning. The school usually called her by seven if someone needed a sub, but this morning, the phone was silent. Caroline began to worry that Shirley would hesitate to call her again, since she had had to leave school on Friday. If that happened, she didn't know what she would do. The school had to have subs who could be expected to come when needed and stay all day, she knew that. She poured herself some more coffee and began to worry over this new coil of events. The phone rang loudly and caused her to jump.

"Finally!" she said aloud, putting the receiver up to her ear. I'll bet Mrs. Turner is out again with her little girl. She has so many ear infections. "Hello?"

"Hello, Caroline! You up?" a cheery male voice spoke loudly to Caroline. "This is Harold Weiss. Sorry to call so early, but I'm going to have to go over to Clover Mills this morning and look over some property. I told Myron I'd drop off his cider mill today and looks like it's going to have to be an early delivery. I probably will be out of town all day. Does 8:30 sound too early?"

"Harold? Lord, I'd forgotten all about Poppy's cider mill. What did you let him buy that thing for? Where are we going to put it? I could wring your neck, Harold!" Caroline laughed, enjoying the sound of his deep voice. "First, you let Coker steal my furniture, then sell my daddy some monstrosity that he'll probably lose a finger in!"

Harold laughed along with Caroline. "Well, Caroline, you know us businessmen, anything for a dollar. Myron was set on having the mill, and it really is in good shape. Seems like I remember Jasper buying it not too long ago. I'm not even sure that he ever used it."

"Um huh, so I'm supposed to be happy that he got a good deal or something," Caroline continued to joke. "Eight-thirty is fine, Harold. I think I hear Poppy getting up now. He will be all excited with his new toy. Harold, I'm going to get off. The high school may be trying to call me this morning, although it's getting a little late. I'll see you in a little while. Drive on around back when you come."

Harold told her he was on his way back over to the Collins' house and he would swing by then. Caroline hung up and called to her father.

"Pop? You up? Harold's on his way with your mill. You'll have to tell him where you want to put the thing. I sure don't know what you're going to do

41

with it!" She looked over her shoulder as her father shuffled into the kitchen, fully dressed except for his shoes.

"Good thing he's getting here early," grunted her father, seating himself at the table. "I think we can run over to the Farmer's Market and get several bushels of apples. I'd like to have some Winesaps, but I imagine they've just got Red Delicious. I wish your mama was here. She could always pick the best apples for cider."

"The Farmer's Market? This morning? No way, Poppy, am I going over there this morning. I can't lift bushels of apples, anyway, and you sure can't. I have to wait and see if the school ca-...."

"Caroline, we have to get started on the cider this afternoon. The apples won't wait. I told your mother that we could wash'em up outside at the spigot and then run 'em through by nightfall. We'll have a good run of fresh press by bedtime."

"No, Poppy. I don't think making a bunch of cider is a good idea. Maybe we can try a little bit with a bushel of apples, but you're talking about a lot of work. What will you do with it? How much do you plan on making? Can't we just get some from the market and try a few at a time?" Caroline didn't know why she was having this conversation. She had hoped that her father would look at the cider mill and decide that he didn't want to fool with it, but of course this didn't happen. Just what I need for the fall. Sticky, buggy apple juice all over my porch and kitchen. The yellow jackets will be swarming everywhere. And he's confused about Mama again. She felt her neck muscles begin to tense.

Her father had stopped talking and was looking at her with the same expression he had had when she was eleven and had told him that she was too old to go out to eat with her parents at the SeaChick Diner. That combination of hurt and disbelief had the same effect on her now as it had then. She couldn't bear it.

"Why, Caroline, I'm surprised at you. You never have turned down a trip to the Farmer's Market and your mama's wanting that cider awful bad. Wait, I'll get her in here." Myron stepped to the back door and pushed open the screen. Caroline watched him sadly as he peered onto the empty porch. Almost immediately, he dropped his head and sheepishly looked back at his daughter.

"Ah, hell, I know she ain't there, Caroline. I'm getting so mixed up lately, what's going on with me?" He shuffled over to his chair and sat down heavily. Caroline saw his hand shake as he picked up his coffee cup.

"It's okay, Poppy, don't worry about it. Maybe I'll call Dr. Anthony today and let him check you out. It's about time for your check up, anyway. We'll just drop in to see him a little earlier than usual." Caroline reached over to squeeze her father's arm.

"Mebbe so," he mumbled into his coffee cup.

Well, thought Caroline to herself. At least he's not thinking about the apples anymore. I'll call Shirley and tell her that I want to be called first thing tomorrow if anyone needs a sub. She reached for the phone just as a truck's horn was heard from outside.

Myron perked up. "That's Harold with the mill! 'Bout time, too. The market closes at twelve on Mondays. We'll have to get a move on, Caroline. Come on, you might have to help Harold unload the thing."

Caroline jumped to her feet. "I'm not lifting anything, Pop. And neither are you. If Harold can't get this thing off his truck, he can take it back with him!" She continued to fume all the way to the driveway for whatever good it did. Myron beat her to Harold's van, grinning from ear to ear as Harold climbed out with a cheery, "Mornin', Myron. Caroline."

"Morning, Harold. You got m'mill? Caroline and I are going over to Vernon to get apples. We should have some juice by nightfall. You'll have to drop by and have a taste."

Caroline stood, arms crossed, and glared at both men. Ridiculous things, grinning like two monkeys. "Harold, if you can't get that thing out of there, you can take it on back with you. I am not throwing my back out on a cider mill, and neither is Poppy. You men, I swear...!"

Harold held up his hands in defense. "Now, Caroline, you know I don't take back what I sell. And not to worry. Carl and I will put the mill wherever you and your dad want it. He waved over his slow-witted cousin, Carl, who often helped him set up his auctions or carry purchased items to cars and trucks. What Carl lacked upstairs, he made up for in physical strength. Carl grinned at Caroline and immediately dropped his head to study the ground. He was shy around women, except for his mother, whom he bossed around like a rooster in the hen house.

"Harold, I've got just enough room for the mill out here in the shed. I was moving a few things around last night. You and Carl won't have to tote it too far." Myron began moving, at a good pace, Caroline noted, toward the old shed that stood back of the garage.

"Okay, Carl, you jump up there and get hold of the mill. It's not really that heavy, just awkward." Harold opened the back of his van and Carl disappeared inside. After much grunting and straining, they had the mill on the ground. Caroline enjoyed watching the play of Harold's muscles tightening against the knit fabric of his shirt as he heaved the mill out of the van. Nice legs, too, she noticed as he and Carl worked their way to the shed. And he's wearing bermudas. She sighed contentedly. Not a bad Monday morning after all. Working men were always a pleasant sight to Caroline.

After some arranging and rearranging, Myron seemed satisfied enough with his delivery to go into the house for his checkbook. Carl had scooted for the van as soon as he could, leaving Caroline and Harold alone in the shed. Caroline looked Harold in the eye.

"You know, Harold, this thing is only going to make a lot of trouble for me. Poppy's dead serious about making cider with it, and the way he has been shifting in and out of reality lately, well, I just wish you had tried to talk him out of it."

"Yeah, I thought about that, Caroline, but it's really not too hard to operate, and Myron seemed so excited about it. I imagine the thrill will wear off after a batch or two. It's in great shape, shouldn't give you any trouble. What about I buy it back from you in a month or two if it gets to be too much? Apples won't be plentiful for very much longer, anyway." Harold studied Caroline's face for a response, and not getting one, added, "Tell you what. I'll run by here tonight on my way back from Clover Mills and see if I can help you all out with your first batch."

Caroline's weary thoughts of carrying, washing, and pressing apples suddenly flitted to taut knit shirts, and she grinned.

"Sure, come on by."

The parking lot at the farmer's market was just beginning to fill up when Caroline and her father drove in. Most of the prospective customers seemed to be older farmers and their wives, looking for late season apples and good buys on sweet potatoes. Caroline drove around for awhile looking for the closest space she could find thinking that her dad would find it hard to walk up to the sheds. As usual, she had no idea what was in her father's head.

"Fer God's sake, Caroline, find a place! The best apples will be gone. I just saw Willy Walters back there with his big Ford truck and that half-baked son of his. They'll have bought out all the Winesaps for that damned apple butter his church churns out every fall!" Myron's face was red and getting redder by the minute. Caroline wheeled the car into the next space she saw and slammed on the brakes in a repeat of yesterday's action at Modern-Mart.

Again Myron's body hurtled forward against his seat belt, but he said nothing, just fumbled with the belt and seemed to bolt out of the car.

Man on a mission, she thought as she got out and locked the car. Looking for her father to help him up the hill toward the apple sheds, she was amazed to see him halfway up the sidewalk, swinging his arms with more energy and life than she had seen in him in awhile. When she caught up with him, he was already moving up and down the aisles, examining the Winesaps, Romes, and Red Delicious with great delight.

"Look 'ahere, Caroline, look at that deep red color on the Winesaps. I think we'll get a bushel of them and one of the Red Delicious. Young lady, can you cut me a slice of each of those apples? Let me see what they taste like?" Myron addressed the young girl who was sitting behind the bushel baskets of fruit.

"Nawsir, my granddaddy told me not to cut any more apples. We done gave away enough free samples today," she answered with a toss of her stringy blond hair.

"Well, goddamn," exclaimed Myron. "I ain't never. Now, how you figure you're going to sell your product if you don't let people see if it's any good? Where's your granddaddy? I want a word with'im."

"He ain't here. He went to get some lunch and he tol' me to not to cut up any more apples. I'm just doing what I was told!" The girl's eyes had widened at Myron's choice of language, had dug in her heels, and was prepared to do battle. Caroline, foreseeing a showdown, pulled at her father's arm and steered him on down the aisle.

"Come on, Poppy, let's look around some more. There may be somebody else with apples already sliced. It is getting to be lunch time. Do you want to go eat now and get some coffee? We can come back to get apples later." Caroline hoped that the thought of lunch at *Grandma's Table*, the café operated by the market, would distract and disarm her father's temper.

"No, we came to buy apples! And I'm going to buy apples! But I want to taste 'em first!" Myron's voice was trembling with anger and had become loud enough to attract the attention of the other shoppers.

"Caroline, can I help you?"

A voice that Caroline knew very well but had not heard for some time caused her to turn quickly. "Tony? Is that you? What are you doing here?"

Tony Mills, everyone's heartthrob from Caroline's high school days, stood grinning sheepishly before them. Tony, talented on the gridiron and the dance floor, and voted Most Likely to Break Hearts, had gone off to a small college to play football after graduation. But life as BMOC in high school had not been as easy on the college scene and he had returned home after a couple of semesters. Caroline rarely saw him around town but had heard of him driving trucks across country and hitting the bottle pretty hard. She smiled sweetly at him noticing his deep brown, rather bloodshot eyes.

"Oh, I help out around here during the fall season. There's not too much cross-country freight going out this time of year. You know, vegetables and stuff. That's what I usually haul. It's good to see you, Caroline. Was there something you and your daddy were lookin' for in particular?" Tony nodded to Myron who was peering closely at him from around Caroline's shoulder. "Evenin', Mr. Arrowood, remember me, Tony Mills? Anson's son." Tony put out his hand to Myron.

"Anson? Anson? Can't recall any Anson's. What'cher last name again?"

"Mills, Tony. Anson Mills is my daddy. He ran the Gulf station downtown. You always brought your Buick in for him to tune up, remember?

A light went on in Myron's eyes. "Gulf station, did'ja say? Well, of course. Your daddy and me used to...well never mind, you young'ns wouldn't need to know all that! How the hell is ol' Anson? I haven't seen him in awhile."

"Well, he's dead, Mr. Arrowood. He died two years ago this Christmas. Lung cancer," Tony glanced at Caroline as she watched her father out of the corner of her eyes. She shook her head briefly at Tony.

The brightness in Myron's eyes changed to confusion and disbelief. "Now when were you going to tell me about Anson, Caroline? Dammit, I'm sorry, young feller. I thought a lot of your dad."

"That's okay, Mr. Arrowood. Now, what did I hear you saying about apples? What kind did you want again?" Tony put his arm around Myron's thin, stooped shoulders and led him on down the aisle. Caroline followed slowly behind offering a silent prayer for the Tonys of this world who dealt gently with the elderly.

"Caroline, just pull around back next to the shed and we'll get these apples out and start our juice before supper. I tell ya', just the smell of those little beauties in the trunk has made me thirsty!" Myron grinned at his daughter. Caroline wasn't grinning back.

"Pa, let's wait until Harold comes by to unload the apples. Tony was nice enough to put them in the back for us, but three bushels of apples are too much for me and you. Harold said he would help us when he comes back from Clover Mills. I need to start supper, anyway. I'm hungry, aren't you?"

I am not about to lift a bushel of apples nor is he going to try and have a stroke in the backyard she swore to herself.

Surprisingly, her father agreed and contented himself to wiping down the cider press and taking small buckets of apples from the car to the old stainless steel sink in the shed to wash them off. Caroline figured that the numerous trips he would have to make between car and sink would soon tire him out and he would stay out of the way when Harold came to unload the car. Glancing out the screen door from time to time as she cooked, she watched him puttering back and forth between the car and the shed and heard him whistling tunelessly.

"Pa. Come on in! I've got salmon cakes and fried potatoes with onions."

Myron appeared in the door of the shed, empty bucket in hand, but lost no time in scuttling across the yard and into his place at the kitchen table. He spooned potatoes onto his plate and then placed two steaming salmon cakes beside them. "Got any ketchup for these cakes?"

Caroline handed him a small bottle of Heinz and he anointed each cake with a healthy squirt of the sauce. A couple of hearty bites finished off one cake; then he started into the potatoes.

"I swear, Caroline, one of the best things your mamma ever did was to teach you to cook. This tastes so good, or maybe I'm just hungry after a hard day's work, you reckon?"

"I'd say a little bit of both, Poppy. Maybe we should have eaten at the Market. Their country style steak looked awfully good."

"Couldn't be better than this. I do love a good salmon cake," Myron declared, finishing off his second cake. "When's what's his name coming by to help with the apples?"

"Harold? He should be here before dark. Now, Pa, I want you to understand something. If this operation gets to be too much for either one of us, Harold has promised to buy the press back from you. It sounds like too much trouble and I..."

"Now, Caroline, you don't know what you're talkin' about. Making cider or good old apple juice won't be the death of you or me. You'll see. The chopper and the press do all the work. We'll need something to catch the juice in. What about that canner your momma had? The blue one with the white spots? Where is that thing?"

"It's in the laundry room along with all of her canning things. I'll get it down and wash it out. Why don't you take your coffee in the den and rest until Harold gets here. I think you can catch the news if you want." Myron shuffled off with his coffee cup in hand and soon she heard the drone of the nightly news. She quickly cleared the table, loaded the dishwasher, and went in search of the canner.

The canner sat on the top shelf above the washing machine, along with an array of Mason and Ball glass jars her mom had used year after year to can tomatoes, okra, and other vegetables from their garden. *I ought to box all this stuff up and give it to Goodwill,* Caroline thought for the one-hundredth time. She had gotten the old step stool from the kitchen and was atop the third step retrieving the canner, when she heard Harold's truck pull in behind her car. She put the canner in the kitchen sink and went to the door.

"Hi, Harold. Thanks for coming by. I know you are ready to get home," Caroline pushed open the screen door. Although there was precious little waiting for him there, Caroline knew. Harold's wife, Laureen, had left him several years back and now lived in Atlanta. People said she met someone on the Internet, but that might have been just gossip. Harold never talked about her.

He stood in her kitchen and smiled down at Caroline. He was a big man, Caroline found herself thinking. Laureen was a fool. Well, maybe people thought that about her for leaving Bobby Ray. No one really knew what went on in other people's lives.

"Have a seat, Harold. I'll get Poppy." Caroline pointed toward her father's chair. "He's been so excited about this apple cider." Stepping into the den, she found her father sound asleep in his recliner, the coffee cup loosely held in his hand and dangerously angled on the arm of the chair. *Damnit, wouldn't you know,* she thought angrily. *I will not take this on by myself!* And she shook her father's shoulder, not gently.

"Poppy, wake up, Harold's here to help with the apples."

"Hunh?? Who? Don't bother me, Caroline, I'm tired!" Myron brushed off her hand and started to snore loudly. He looked so old and worn out that she gave up.

"Harold, looks like it's you and me for Apple Cider 101. Poppy's down for the count. I knew he was doing too much today." Caroline stepped back into the kitchen.

Harold grinned and stood up. "That's okay. I'd rather teach you about cider making than your father anyway. Is there a light in that shed out back?"

Caroline laughed. "Yes, there's a light and a lot more apples to unload. I told you that you were going to regret selling that thing to my daddy." She held the door open for him and they walked toward the car.

Harold glanced at the remaining baskets of apples. Pulling one basket toward him, he lifted it easily out of the trunk. "I don't regret a thing, Caroline, not yet, anyway," he smiled, sending her a wink.

Sandman, send me a dream, Caroline sang to herself. She followed Harold into the shed.

Vignettes

Mary stood on the porch still in her nightgown with bare feet. She thought, *I ought to feel somethin'! To cry or somethin'.* But she didn't cry as she watched Pete leave in the wagon with his father. He sat very straight and tall on the seat, his canvas WWI issue rucksack stowed behind the seat. She could just make out the cowlick in the back of his dark hair as the wagon slowly creaked up the dirt road and then out of sight. Her feet were freezing and beginning to ache. This, not tears, drove her inside the house to the warmth of the cook stove.

Mary lifted the heavy cast iron skillet from its hook on the wall and placed it on the stove top. *Kids'll be up soon. I'll have to tell them their Pa's gone, gone to the crazy house. Jim'll miss him most but Hannah won't. And I won't neither! If I never see him again, it'll be just fine.*

The ham was sizzling and had loaned its rich brown color to the eggs Mary had turned over when a sleepy voice asked. "Where'd Pa go, Ma? I heard Grandpa outside with the wagon. Where'd they go?"

Mary moved the skillet off the stove eye and turned to face her 11 year old son standing in the kitchen doorway. Bone thin, hair the color of old straw, Jim's face held a wary, worried look.

"Yore grandpa's takin' Pa to Marion, son. He's sick, Jim. He can't stay here no more. Not after last week. It's not safe."

"Wal, will he get better? When will he be back? What'd yuh let Grandpa take him for, Ma? I could'a watched him fer yuh. Me and Pa get along just fine! Pa didn't mean anything last week. He just got mad!" Jim threw himself into a caned bottom kitchen chair and began to cry.

Mary watched Jim with sadness. *A good mother would tell Jim that everything will be all right*, she told herself. *A good mother would put her arms around her child and wipe away those tears, but I can't do that.*

"Now, Jim. There ain't no use in crying. Yore Pa nearly killed us last week setting that fire. I can't trust him not to hurt me and Hannah. I know he never hurt you, but son, he told me he was sorry me and Hannah hadn't died and he would kill us next chance he got. Your Grandpa heard him say that and said he'd better take him to Marion. They left early because it's a long way. You'll have to be the man of the house now and help out. I can't run this farm by mys....

"Shut up!" screamed Jim, leaping to his feet and shoving Mary back against the stove edge. She caught Jim by the upper arms and retrieved her balance.

"Jim, calm down. Grandpa can talk to you when he gets back. He'll tell us all about what the doctors say about your Pa! Maybe they can make him well...."

Jim shoved past Mary and was out the door, his tears becoming uncontrollable sobs. Mary watched him through the open door as he headed across the yard and to the barn. Let him go, she told herself. The animals will calm him.

Mary got a plate from the cabinet over the sink and filled it with two eggs and a slice of ham. She moved into the dining room and sat in Pete's chair. Might as well sit here, she thought. He won't be back to use it.

She suddenly was very hungry. The salty flavor of the ham and eggs was delicious and Mary ate it all. She could feel the nourishment move into her body and, it seemed into her soul.

Old Debts

Dear Father,

I enclose you $10.00. You can pay Mr. Eaton what I owe him. I think I owe Mr. Eaton about seven dollars. You can find out what it is. Tell Mr. Eaton to send me the amount of my account and also send me receipt for the amount you pay him. I will pay him the remainder just as soon as I can. Hope you are getting along all right. I will send you all the money I possibly can this summer.

James tilted back in the hard straight backed chair that he had pulled up to Mr. Austin's desk and sighed loudly. "I know that I owe that money to Mr. Eaton, but I'll be damned if I send it all at once. He has enough money, more than anyone back home-old miser! Wasn't my doing anyway-he'll just have to wait for the rest of the thirty. Dexter oughta have to pay somethin'-he's the one that broke into the store anyway."

James closed his eyes and the whole night of July 9, 1884 replayed itself in his head. The wild buggy ride to Pearisburg, the hard liquor that Dex had bought from old man Raines, the sweat on Fanny's flanks as Dexter slashed her with the whip headed back to Sugar Run and Eaton's store. He remembered the demonic smile on Dex's face as he broke out the front windows in the store with a large creek rock, and his own dizzied entry into the front door. "Hell, I begged Dex to stop, that Mr. Eaton would know who had broke up his store, but he just kept on his tear, rantin' about Sally and her daddy not lettin' Sally marry him. Dex was drunk and I was too, but still... who's working to pay off that mess? Me, that's who. Dex is somewhere in Roanoke, lyin' low. Father would never let Mr. Eaton put him in jail. I know he knows where Dex is, probably helped him get there. And here I am, stuck in Austin's Dry Goods, working hard and sending as much as I can home. Damn Dex. Damn Father, too. He always stuck up for Dexter even though he knew that I liked Sally better than Dex. Dex didn't care enough for any woman."

James shook his head and took up his pencil again remembering Dex's last words before Father took him off in the buggy the next night. "Bye, little brother, and don't forget. It's no good chasin' after women. They always ruin ya." His father cracked the whip and Fanny trotted quickly out into the dark night, her hooves sounding rhythmically on the dirt road until he couldn't hear them anymore.

I guess you got your hat by this time. If so, how do you like it? Write at once and let me know if you rec'd the money and the hat also. Love to all.

Your affectionate son, J. Tyler

(Two months later)

James sat again at Mr. Austin's desk and opened the letter that had arrived that morning

July 10, 1886

Dear Son,

Rec'd your letter of May 6. Money was delivered as you asked and the hat arrived in good shape. Mr. Austin's store sure stocks good hats keeps the sun off my head real good. Mr. Eaton seems to have settled down about the damage you and Dexter laid on his store and has stopped threatening the law on me. As long as you send me the rest of the money by the end of the summer, I reckon things will come around alright.

Crops are pretty good this summer. Tomatoes and beans have got the beetle, but we manage to get some tomatoes for dinner. Taters might make a small crop in September.

I enclose a clipping from the Staffordsville Record. I knew you would want to know what has settled Mr. Eaton down some. If I can, your mother and I will take a trip down your way next month.

Your loving father.

"Miss Ruth Garrett entertained at a tea on Saturday afternoon, at her home in Orchard Heights, where she announced the engagement of Miss Sally Eaton to Mr. Dexter Meadows of Roanoke, Virginia. Miss Eaton is the daughter of John and Betsy Eaton of Sugar Run. Mr. Meadows is the son of Sam and Eliza Meadows of Wabash. A December wedding is planned at Eaton's Chapel in Thessalia, Virginia. The couple plan to live in Roanoke where Mr. Meadows is employed by The National Bank of Roanoke." (**Staffordsville Record**, Saturday, June 10, 1886.)

James crumpled the letter and crammed it into his vest pocket.

"That tears it! Dexter is a skunk of the first water. Well, I'm not going to the wedding. They better not ask me. I'd probably kill him! Father will play hell getting any more money from me. Let the banker pay his daddy-in-law! Hell with the whole bunch! I hope Sally enjoys her new husband. Low-life, no good....!"

Mr. Austin looked up from his accounts to watch his young employee as he muttered and strode back and forth behind the store's long counter. When James viciously kicked at the store's old black and white cat who chose that time to cross his path, the old man spoke up.

"Now, James, whatever has got your dander up, I don't think kicking old Toby is going to help anything. What is wrong with you?"

James stopped his pacing and glared at his employer. "It's this damned letter from my father about my brother! He's getting married!"

"Well, now that's a fine thing, idn't it? Who's he marrying? Anyone you know?" Mr. Austin smiled at James. "Does she have a sister for you, mebbe?"

"Mr. Austin, this is not a happy thing. My brother is the reason I had to leave home, get a job, and now he is doing just dandy, getting married and all. Oh, I'm mad enough to bite a nail in two!" James ran his hand over his hair and covered his eyes. He felt like crying.

"Mr. Austin, do you think I could take the rest of the afternoon off? I've got to go see my brother. This marriage has thing has just set me back. I can be back on time in the morning," James implored.

"It'll be all right, long as you are on time tomorrow. How're you going to get there? The train's already left for Roanoke."

James jammed his fists in his pockets. "Don't reckon you would lend me your buggy? I could pay you out of this week's wages."

"I figured that would be the next question," Mr. Austin growled. "Yes, you can borrow the buggy and Jack. Just be sure you feed him good when you get to Roanoke. There's a good stable on Winter Street. Ask for Mr. Adams. He'll rub Jack down good and give him some good feed. Now don't you be forcing him to go too fast. He ain't as young as he used to be!"

"Winter Street, did you say?" James went for his coat and hat from the hall tree in the corner. "I'll see you in the morning."

"Now wait a minute, young devil. Where is your brother? Do you have his address?"

James grinned wickedly. "No, I do not, but I know where he works—at the National Bank of Roanoke! And I plan to drop in and do a little business with Mr. Dexter Meadows. Thanks again, Mr. Austin. See you tomorrow."

James made his way to the stable and hurriedly got Jack between the buggy's traces. His hands trembled as he carefully harnessed the horse and climbed onto the narrow seat. The blacksnake whip with its braided handle quivered in its metal holder as James picked up the reins. James stared at the whip and removed it slowly. Whips are evil things, he thought to himself and snapped it forward right above Jack's ears. The horse jumped forward with a snort of surprise. James laughed.

"Don't worry Jack. I'm not using this whip on *you*. But it's going to get used and rightly so, in my opinion!"

James headed the buggy onto the mountain road leading to Roanoke and revenge.

Grandma Sallie

Roanoke, Virginia
June, 1919

Dear Riley and family,
I will write you a few lines. Gotten your letter just before I mailed my letter. I am feeling very good this morning. Eat biscuits and gravy. Can turn in bed little better then I did seems like I have been here one year. I cannot write good lying on my back. Come if you can come. I would love to see all of you. It goes awful hard with me to be away from you all so long but my pains has gone. Tell Elise have a pot of green beans when I get there. Wish I had good drink milk from home. I have written enough write often
From your mother one who loves you. Tell Randall <u>want to see him awful bad</u> Tell him to be good.

Elise folded the letter in thirds and put it back in the envelope marked to "Riley Albert and Family, Staffordsville, Virginia." The little boy sat close to his mother and held out his hand to hold the letter.

"Grandma Sallie is gettin' better, Momma?" he asked. His grey eyes, so like his mother's, filled with worry and caused his mother to pull him even closer to her side.

"Yes, Randall, she is gettin' better. See, she was able to write this letter to us and wants a pot of green beans when she gets home. She's had an awful time with her gall bladder, but the operation will make her better. When she gets home, we'll pick a mess of beans and take it up on the hill. Now you be good, like she says until I get the dishes cleaned up. Then you can go find your daddy at the store. See if Mr. Joe has some peppermints. I think I have a penny or two for good little boys."

Elise gave her little boy a kiss on his forehead and went to the well to get some water for dishes. Randall sat back on the horsehair sofa and continued to look at the letter. He pulled it back out of the envelope and studied his grandmother's words. The letters and words looked like the fine dust outside of the chicken coop when the hens scratched lines and grooves as they looked for insects. He knew what words were and he understood

56

what letters were. Sometimes they came to the house and made his mother very happy and sometimes they came and made her very sad. One day when he was older, he would write letters to his momma and they would just make her happy. He didn't like her to be sad and cry like she did when daddy made her unhappy with things he said. He loved his momma very much. Daddy frightened him and he was glad when he left to go to sit at the store. He had been to the store with his daddy and he didn't see why the men wanted to sit there all day. He liked to go to the store and get a piece of stick candy when it was bought for him, but he got so tired standing beside his daddy while the men talked, talked, talked, laughed at things he didn't understand, and spat on the old stove. He didn't like the smell of the tobacco juice and spit as it ran down the hot stove and he was always ready to go home long before his daddy would take him.

"Mamma," he called when he heard her come back into the kitchen. "Will Daddy go to Ro'noke to see Grandma Sallie? Can we go, too?"

"I don't think we can all take the train. It would cost too much. He might go when she is ready to come home. Great Pa will probably need some help bringing her home. I bet you'd like the train ride. Maybe we can go at Christmas to see Uncle Tyler and Aunt Minnie. Would you like that?

"Yeah, but I want to see Grandma Sallie soon. I miss her." Ralph closed his eyes and thought of his grandma's short, heavy figure. He really did want her to hurry home. He missed her cooking and just her very self. He loved to sit on her lap. She was so soft and comfortable. Sometimes after Sunday dinner, he would climb up on her lap and she would rock him to sleep. Full of fried chicken, gravy and biscuits, he could barely hold his eyes open to hear her stories.

And her stories were just the best! Sometimes she would tell him stories about cowboys and Indians of the western states and other times she would tell him things his daddy had done when he was a little boy. (He could never picture his daddy as a little boy, but grandma said he was "full of himself" as she put it and "never missed a beat.")

But her ghost stories were his very favorite, although he usually had to spend the night in bed with his mother and daddy after she told him one. It seemed like the very minute he got in his little bed upstairs in the cabin by the creek, all those wild buggy rides, evil horses and traveling gypsies that his grandmother had told him about hovered over him and sent him screaming down the stairs to his mother's bed. Once he was snugly tucked in between his mom and dad, he could conjure all those scary things back up and relive them with just a few goose bumps rising on his arms.

He thought then about the last story she had told him before she left for the hospital. In the daylight, it didn't seem like much, but hearing his grandma tell it that night had made his hair stand on end.

"Well, it was a warm summer night when your grandpa and me was acourtin'. We had gone to the Christian church down there by your house for prayer meetin' and we was aridin' back up to my house up there on the hill, don't you know. I was ridin' Brownie, my mare, and your granddaddy was on his horse, King. Well, it had gotten quite dark while we was in church but the moon was as big as a punkin and just as bright. We didn't need no lantern. Your granddaddy was wantin' me to go slow so he could steal a kiss, but I told him I had to get home. My mama didn't want me out late so we rode at a right steady pace a'talkin' and a' laughin'. When we got to the first turn up Staffordsville Hill we heard a horseman coming up behind us at a pretty good clip. Well sir, George turned in his saddle to greet the rider and suddenly this horse and rider rode in between us. It was a man, oh, I guess about 50 or so, with a military hat on his head. He was aridin' a large black horse who snorted and pranced as he came between our two mounts. I spoke to the gentleman, "Good evenin', Sir," I said. George said, "Were you at the prayer meetin', Sir?" But he never said a word to us, just rode along quiet like, looking straight ahead, and don't you know he made me nervous. And Brownie didn't like it, not one bit. I had a time keeping her under control. She snorted and tossed her head. And King was doing the same thing on the left of the man. Well sir, we rounded the bend at the Moye's house and topped the hill and just as suddenly as that rider appeared, he disappeared, like smoke. Me and George stopped our horses right in the middle of the road and looked all around, but the horse and his rider was just not there anymore. I tell you, Randall, you never saw any two people high tail it any faster on up to my daddy's house. It makes me shiver just to think of it now. People told us later that we had ridden past the cemetery and conjured up a ghost, a Civil War ghost. Coulda been, I guess. We never rode that way again at night, I want you to know."

Ralph folded his grandmother's letter very carefully and put it back in the envelope. Maybe she would be home soon and could tell him about her stay in the hospital. Maybe that man came to see her in the hospital. Wouldn't that be strange? Suddenly, it was too much to think about. Randall threw the letter down on the kitchen table and ran out of the cabin and straight up the crooked little path to the road. He was so glad it was day light because *that* road was the same one Grandma Sallie and Great Pa were on when the stranger rode in between them. Shivers ran up the little boy's back and he sped as fast as he could to the store. For once he would be glad to see his stern daddy, the men with their grinning faces and tobacco stained mouths. They suddenly seemed beautiful to him. He hoped he wouldn't cry when they looked at him.

To Drive

I think some of the most emotional and heart-tugging music and lyrics reside in the world of country music. If you are feeling low, weepy or just downright want to have a pity party for yourself, there is a line or "hook", as they refer to their catchy lines, just for you. Or, if you want to laugh out loud there are plenty that can do that too. Alan Jackson, for example, can evoke memories for me that can make me sob out loud or create a giggle deep in my belly that has to be shared.

One of those songs which I think he wrote just for me is "Drive". If you are not a C&W aficionado, the song begins with the singer's memories of an old plywood boat that his daddy bought when he was a young boy. Nothing special, he says, just a 75 Johnson, electric choke. But the beauty comes when daddy lets him drive. A young boy, he says, two hands on the wheel, he can't replace the way it made him feel.

I have to agree when I remember driving my daddy's light blue Chrysler to the country store by myself for the first time. That act created such a feeling of power, freedom and joy that I, like Jackson, cannot replace with *any* other experience in my life. Was I careful, oozing down that curvy little two-lane, slowing down at each turn like I had done when driving with my parents? Of course not. I tried that old baby out, making the tires squeal and riding the brakes into each mountain switchback. As another country song suggests, Wild Angels must have been watching over me on my trip to the store and back. In my defense, I must add that this did not lead to a life of speeding and accidents. I left that to my brother and sisters, but that first taste of freedom behind a wheel was intoxicating. I wouldn't trade it for anything.

Unlike the youth of today, my age group did not get a car of their own upon turning 16. We had a family car (one) that had to used primarily to get my daddy to work and mamma to the grocery store once a week. By the time I was driving, my brother had his own car and my sisters were both on their own with vehicles, so when I ventured out of the country to town for dances, ballgames or to the Dari Delight to flirt and meet friends, it was a rare and precious occasion. As often as Alan may have gotten to drive, my daddy did not consider it a God-given right to use the car. I had had my license about a month when the Homecoming Bonfire rolled around. I thought it would be fun to drive myself and a friend to the high school and watch the goings-on as the cheerleaders shouted and jumped and the hunky football players stood around in their monogram jackets and sneered at the silly creatures all the while giving each other "frogs" in each other's biceps. I nervously slunk into the garden where Poppy was pulling up corn stalks to make into "shocks".

"Poppy, could I have the car to go the bonfire tonight?" I asked, timidly, knowing what the answer would be.

"I don't think so. You haven't been driving very long," he answered, never looking at me as he continued to pull and stack the golden brown stalks in place.

I huffed and puffed my way back into the house and to my room. No bonfire for me that night except inside myself as I raged against parents, living out in the sticks and no boyfriend to escort me here thither and yon. Daddy *didn't* let me drive and rightly so.

But there were other times when the answer was yes. I was the last of the four children to drive Ralph's cars and I think he was tired of raising Mario Andretti wannabes, so he kind of gave up when I was behind the wheel. He never raised his voice or told me what to do, unlike my husband today even though I have been driving for about 50 years. Once, I was driving us back home from town, with my brother in the back and Poppy in the passenger's seat. I can't for the life of me remember why I was driving, but Daddy let me drive. We were driving slowly past the home of one of my old flames who chose this time to come out of his house and vault himself into his convertible Jeepster. It caught my attention, to say the least. We were in a line of slow moving traffic which I had completely forgotten about. I felt, rather than heard my father's quick intake of breath and I looked back to see the back end of the car in front of us extremely close to us, too close. I slammed on brakes and screeched to a halt just in time. Embarrassing is too small a word. My sweet old man just said calmly, "You have to keep your eyes on the road, all the time."

Nowadays, the right to drive and my abilities to do so are taken for granted each time I slide behind the wheel. I go where I want, when I want and never have to ask permission. Although that overpowering feeling of joy that I felt at 16 never happens anymore, this winter I did stop to realize what I would be giving up when I can no longer tool myself around. After having a few seizures in January and dizziness all through February, I was very cautious about driving my car and had to be transported everywhere or stay at home. It is truly confining to rely on others to get you about. Slowly

I recuperated to the point that I felt safe driving and felt others to be safe from me! I will not take that right for granted again and I confidently went in to the DMV to renew my license the other week.

"Have you had any health problems lately-suffered unconsciousness, had seizures, passed out?" asked the DMV employee. (The staff at DMVs still scare me to death.)

"No, ma'am," I answered and she let me drive.

To drive: To be free, joyous and in control. Use it wisely.

Sick Beds I Have Known

I spent most of Saturday and Sunday in bed, having been ambushed by yet another attack of diverticulitis. As I lay there groaning (I tend to groan when I don't feel well), I began to think of the many sickbeds I have known over the years. That, of course, conjured up the caregivers I have had and the care that I have given, on occasion.

Naturally, I thought of the many times I was cared for by my mother. I grew up in the mountains of Southwest Virginia in the '50's and everyone heated their homes with coal furnaces, mine being no exception. My entire family suffered monumental headaches and sinus problems probably due to this dusty, although warm type of heat. I did not have the headaches but we all had the "flu" every year. And sometimes we had the "old timey flu" which entailed a bad head cold, cough and stomach upsets as well. It was never a happy time, but it could all be made better by taking to Mama's bed downstairs. Our upstairs bedrooms lacked heat, an expense eschewed by my daddy who believed in the scientific principle of heat rising. Well, we paid him back in spades because as soon as he had gone to work, we moved our infectious little selves into their bed and he invariably caught what we had. Mama, on the other hand, rarely got sick, nursing us night and day. It is ironic that she died 22 years before my dad who stayed healthy as a horse for most of those 22 years.

When I was in the fourth grade, I was stricken with scarlet fever. I was ill all night, taken to the doctor for a powerful shot of penicillin with one of those long awful hypodermic needles they used back then and felt much better right away. However, I was quarantined for two weeks. Mama had my bed moved into the little den off her bedroom. This was a sunny, cozy little room with a picture window and plenty of heat as long as the door was open from their bedroom. There I recuperated for two weeks, writing letters to my best friend, Sue, and getting very irritable with having to stay away from school which I dearly loved. What a sweet woman my mother was! She brought me meals and read to me at night. I hope I thanked her, but bet I didn't. She belonged to the Home Demonstration Club in our community, an arm of the Extension Service at Virginia Tech. In this little club, the women had learned how to make a hospital bed, nurse the sick and cook special dishes. Any time we were sick, Mama went off to buy ginger ale and lime sherbet. I never liked lime sherbet, but Mama loved it. It probably made her happy when I turned it down, so she could eat some of it. Cheap nurse's wages, I'd say. And through her administrations, by age nine, I knew how to make a hospital corner, pleat the top sheet so that the invalid would not have his feet cramped and how to change the bed without disturbing the patient very much. Mama loved her club.

Now that sick bed was the last time I got really special treatment, but scarlet fever was a serious illness back then and I guess I warranted the attention. Later measles, mumps, more flu usually resulted in trips to Mama's bed and more sicknesses thrust upon my father who was also a groaner. What can I say? It makes us feel better.

Needless to say that my mother was the best caretaker I ever had and my husband is about the worst. This I say with all the love that I can muster for him. It is truly not his fault that he tends to view the patient from the doorway and tries his best to stay as far away as possible from any illness. He is the opposite from me when he is ill. He wants to be left entirely alone and suffer in complete silence. I've rarely heard *him* groan and he usually asks for very little. As I was coddled as a child and the baby of the family, he was *not* coddled as the oldest of three children. He said his mother would always get him a ginger ale if he was sick, but his family tends to ignore sickness in their own family. Someone else always needs more sympathy. For these reasons, he leaves me alone "letting me rest". One day I will show him and just slip away. Then he'll be sorry.

Understand that this tirade comes on the heels of my not being up to par for about four days. I will get over it and bounce back, I hope. While I am mulling over the injustices done to me, I can think of one other horrible caregiver. I had given birth to my second son in 1979 and the luck of the draw had given me a hospital worker who conjured up to me the character of Sary Gamp in **Nicholas Nickleby**, by Charles Dickens. Sary was a "nurse" brought in to help with the dying. She actually was nothing more than an evil woman who sat with her friend dividing up the old man's belongings to make off with when he actually kicked the bucket. This aide or LPN (which I seriously doubt) alighted on me and massaged my poor stomach with a heavy hand. When I groaned (well, of course I did) she informed me that it had to be done. Sary Gamp, I thought. Does she want to take the baby or my nightgowns? Not a good sickbed.

But what of my caregiving? How am I as a nurse, caregiver? Well, I think I do a pretty good job. I have raised two children, cleaned up their upchucks (no child knows how to get out of the bed, run to the toilet, and vomit neatly into the bowl), tolerated drunks and hangovers, taken temperatures, orally and anally. I think I am pretty good. Do I enjoy it? Well....it's okay. I'm always glad when everyone feels better.

My mother spent many days in the hospital before she died. I don't think I was much help to her because she was so sick. But we were a family that feared the hospital and rushed to be with mama when she was there. There are several visits that we would all laugh about, because my mom and dad found other people so amusing. Once, Mama was in a ward with three other women. One lady was visited by four or five friends and her husband. My dad told about the group telling the lady that "Jim" had died recently. Her husband wondered if he could get Jim's hearing aid. "I feel like I'm down in a barrel when people talk to me," he announced. We laughed for years about Jim's hearing aid. And at another time, a lady with two broken legs fell out of her bed-don't ask me how-and all the women including her had a hysterical laughing fit. But the final years for my Mom were nothing to laugh about. My little caregiver deserved better.

My husband's grandmother spent many a year in nursing homes. She usually had a roommate. One, I remember, was paralyzed from a stroke or multiple strokes. She could talk and move her head. She asked me once to wash her face which I did gently with a warm cloth. "Honey," she said, "don't be afraid to rub my face. You can't hurt me." How sad that she used this to be touched and tended to. I'm sure that she was fed, mouth wiped, but rarely kissed, hugged, or just touched. I never saw anyone visit her. Not a pretty sickbed or one any of us wants.

Let's hope for a cozy little bed in a sunny room surrounded by loved ones who have *come in from the doorway* to see us off. A few roses would be nice, too. I like yellow ones. Is that too much to ask?

Printed in the United States
By Bookmasters